The No. 2 **FELINE** Detective Agency

THE TABBY IN BLACK

MANDY MORTON

Farrago

This edition published in 2026 by Farrago,
an imprint of Duckworth Books Ltd
1 Golden Court, Richmond TW9 1EU, United Kingdom

www.farragobooks.com

Printed and bound in Great Britain by Clays Ltd, Elcograf S.p.A.

The authorised representative in the EEA is Easy Access System Europe, Mustamäe tee 50, 10621 Tallinn, Estonia.

Print ISBN: 9781788425940
e-ISBN: 9781788425957

Praise for The No. 2 Feline Detective Agency series

'**Original and intriguing...** a world without people which cat lovers will enter and enjoy.' P. D. James

'**Deliciously clever and a true delight**.' Laura Thompson

'**I loved it.** The whole concept is just so "real"!' Barbara Erskine

'Mandy Morton's Feline Detective Agency instigates a new genre, both **wonderful and surreal**.' Maddy Prior

'There's **so much heart** in this book as well as a **cracking good plot**. Can't wait for the next one!' Barbara Nadel

'The world that Morton has created is **irresistible**.' *Publishers Weekly*

'Witty and smart. **Prepare to be besotted**.' M. K. Graff

'Mandy Morton's series is both **charming and whimsical**.' Barry Forshaw

'Hettie Bagshot might be a new face at the scene of a crime, but already **she could teach most fictional detectives a thing or two**.' *The Hunts Post*

What readers are saying about the series:

'**This** series is **the perfect warm, fluffy cosy mystery read** for fans of Agatha Crispy-style mysteries and cat-lovers alike.'

'**True escapism into a world of pies, cakes and cats** while somehow smuggling a truer reflection of the real world than much human detective fiction.'

'A deceptively nasty murder wrapped up in a cardigan, and served by the fire with tea and cake. **A delight from beginning to end**.'

'**Hilarious and captivating**.'

'**The cat world's answer to the cosy crime novel**, with bags of charm and characters you don't want to leave behind.'

'**I love this series** and am waiting with a warmed pastry, a hot mug of something, and a crackling fire for the next in the series.'

Catberry Family Tree

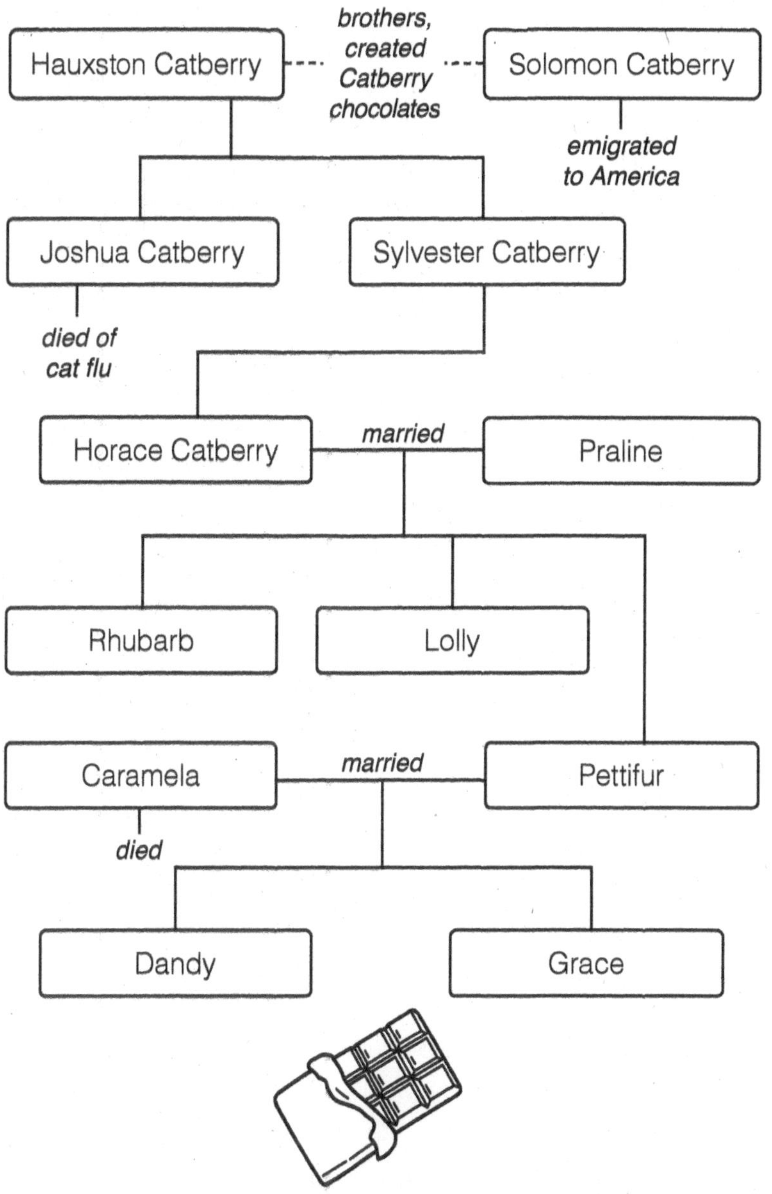

Chapter One

It had been a long, wet spring. In fact, the cats in the town had barely forsaken their firesides since Christmas, only venturing out for essentials during the brief moments when the rain actually stopped. It would be true to say that Meridian Hambone had done a roaring trade in umbrellas, wellingtons and pac-a-macs in her hardware store, but the rest of the businesses in the high street had suffered. Betty and Beryl Butters' bakery had ticked over at a very slow pace; Elsie Haddock had decided to open for fish and chips at teatime only, as her lunchtime trade had dwindled; Hilda Dabbit had closed her dry cleaners and gone on a cruise, hoping for some sunshine; and even Lavender Stamp had been forced to close her post office, as she'd been sent away on a customer awareness course by her head office due to a spate of complaints about her rudeness at the counter. Malkin and Sprinkle, the town's department store, had continued their January sale well into March, greatly reducing their bargains in the hope of attracting some customers but all was in vain as the rain continued.

The No. 2 Feline Detective Agency, run by Hettie Bagshot and Tilly Jenkins from the back room of the Butters' bakery, had all but sunk into a slough of despond. Hettie and Tilly were even considering hanging up their business macs and going on a sightseeing trip with Bruiser in their motorbike and sidecar. Bruiser lived at the bottom of the Butters' garden in a purpose-built shed, and was the driver and muscle to Hettie and Tilly's detective agency. The three cats had shared many an adventure and solved a number of high-profile murder cases in their time together, but now it was as if their world had stopped turning as the rain returned day after day, filling the puddles and drenching any cat brave enough to poke a nose out of the door.

Tilly sat on her fleecy blanket by the fire, fitting the final piece of her Top Cat jigsaw into place. 'That's it, then,' she said, sitting back to enjoy the picture. 'I've done all my jigsaws, read all my Miss Crispy books again and finished the painting by numbers you got me for Christmas – and it's still raining.'

'Not much chance of it stopping, either,' said Hettie, puffing on her catnip pipe. 'I suppose we could join Betty and Beryl on "slug watch" tomorrow for a bit of fresh air. Betty is really upset about them eating all her spring flowers and Beryl's threatening to put the snails in a pie to stop them munching on her pansy pots.'

'I'm not sure I'd like a snail pie – slimy things, and what would you do with the shells?' mused Tilly, leaving her jigsaw to put the kettle on. 'Those French cats eat snails all the time according to Delia Sniff on the TV but I wouldn't want to try one.'

'Well, thankfully we've got a Butters' steak and kidney pie each for our supper,' said Hettie, 'without a snail in sight – and there's a bag of salt and vinegar crisps to go with them.'

'We're so lucky to live behind Betty and Beryl's bakery and getting a pie every day as part of our rent is manna from heaven,' said Tilly, preparing two mugs of milky tea. 'When I was homeless, I used to dream of having a Butters' pie. I used to watch cats eating them in the street, hoping they might abandon one in a bin, but I never got lucky. Now all my dreams have come true. I have a lovely home, a fire, a daily pie and a good friend to share it all with.'

If Hettie hadn't been a long-haired tabby, Tilly might have noticed that she was blushing. Hettie rarely showed her feelings, but there was no doubt that Tilly was her best friend and soulmate. The two cats had met one cold Christmas Eve; Tilly had been frozen and starving in a shop doorway and Hettie had taken her back to her room behind the bakery to warm up; from that day onwards, they had been inseparable.

'I think I'll put the TV on,' said Tilly, passing a mug of tea to Hettie, who had barely stirred from her armchair all day. 'The weather cat will be on in a minute. Maybe they'll have some good news.'

The two tabbies settled down with their tea as the weather cat loomed into view, but the chart behind him told the same dismal story as it had for several weeks. Apologetically, he stuck his rain cloud symbols all over his map, making it clear that the wet weather was here to stay.

'Bloody marvellous!' said Hettie. 'No one in their right mind would want to be out in that, not even murderers, so it looks like we've got at least another week of bad weather and no cases to work on. That telephone in the sideboard hasn't rung since Christmas.'

'But you hate it when it rings,' Tilly pointed out. 'You're always saying that it encroaches on your personal space, which is why you make me answer it.'

'That's because I never know who's on the other end and I don't like surprises.'

Tilly giggled at her friend's reasoning. She was more than used to Hettie's peculiarities and took most of them with a pinch of salt. Hettie was an introvert and surprisingly shy, which her often bad-tempered bluster did a great job of hiding, but Tilly had learnt to see through all the nonsense to the real cat behind the protective mask.

Hettie picked up the *Daily Snout* she'd abandoned on the floor earlier and turned to the TV guide, hoping to find something to lift their spirits. 'Looks like football all evening on both sides, although why they think watching a bunch of cats kicking a ball round a muddy field is entertaining I don't know. After the matches are over, we then have to endure another half hour of why they lost by a load of cats too old to play any more. If we could just get over that one moment of glory when we won the World Cup and accept that we're rubbish at the game, maybe the TV companies might invest in some decent dramas instead of boring us to tears with these amateur kickabouts.'

'I could put a Miss Marble video on,' suggested Tilly, 'although we've watched most of them twice since Christmas, so it's a case of "whodunnit again". Or we could play Scrabble?'

Hettie was about to offer her not-so-complimentary thoughts on Tilly's understanding of the word game and her unique way of spelling when the sideboard suddenly came to life. The telephone, nestled in several cushions, cut through the prospect of any further discussion. Tilly responded immediately and fought her way through the tangle of blankets, cushions and other everyday items to retrieve the phone before it stopped ringing.

'Hello, The No. 2 Feline Detective Agency, Tilly speaking, how may I help?' she said into the receiver, as Hettie sat up in her chair and stretched to turn the TV down, unusually keen to know who might be on the other end. Tilly reached for her notepad and pencil, balancing the phone under her chin, then scribbled some details down as the caller outlined their problem.

The call was soon over and finished with Tilly agreeing to meet up with the potential client the following day at two p.m. She pushed the phone back into the sideboard as Hettie waited impatiently for news.

'So come on,' said Hettie. 'Who was that?'

'It was Pettifur Catberry, calling from Catberry Manor,' said Tilly, trying to contain her excitement. 'You know, the one who owns the chocolate factory out at Catberry-on-the-Brink. They've found some bodies in one of the chocolate vats while they were cleaning it out and he wants us to investigate. We're to meet him at Catberry Manor tomorrow at two.'

'How many bodies?' asked Hettie. 'Sounds pretty ridiculous unless it was suicide by chocolate.'

'He didn't say but he thinks they might have been murdered and dumped in the chocolate.'

'Well, it certainly sounds interesting and I've always wanted a guided tour of that factory. Catberry Manor is worth a look too. Didn't one of those Catberrys die recently?'

'Yes – old Mr Catberry. They had a huge funeral and it was all over the front page of the paper. I think he choked on one of his own Mog Nobs.'

'Marginally better than drowning in a vat of chocolate, I suppose, but what a way to go. Come to think of it, I haven't had a Mog Nob for years. I used to love dipping them in a cup of milky tea.'

'My favourite is their Tabby in Black selection,' said Tilly, filling the kettle again and switching it on, 'mainly because of the advert on TV where he jumps out of a helicopter or dives off a cliff and delivers a box of chocolates to that white fluffy cat through her bedroom window. I'm sure she's the same cat on the liver pâté advert who has no teeth so I don't know how she manages the chocolates with nuts in.'

'And all because the lady loves The Tabby in Black,' said Hettie, mimicking the advert, 'although there are too many creams for my liking and that dark chocolate can be a bit bitter. Give me a Furry Milk selection any day.'

'Oh look,' said Tilly, waving her paw at the TV, 'it looks like that football match has been rained off. They've put a *Tom and Jerry* on instead. Shall we have our pies now and watch it?'

'Sounds like a plan. You sort the pies out and I'll build up the fire and go and let Bruiser know that we've got a job on for tomorrow.'

'It will be lovely to have a run out in Miss Scarlet,' said Tilly, putting the pies on plates and opening the crisps. 'We haven't been out for ages. I hope she hasn't seized up.'

Hettie fetched her mac and pulled on her wellingtons. 'Bruiser would never let that happen,' she said. 'He's motorbike mad and he loves Miss Scarlet almost as much as you do.'

Hettie splashed her way up the Butters' garden to Bruiser's shed and found him enjoying a pie of his own. The shed was warm and cosy and Hettie was pleased to be out of the rain for a few minutes. 'Looks like we've got a new case,' she said. 'There's trouble at the chocolate factory in Catberry-on-the-Brink – bodies in a vat of chocolate, evidently.'

'Blimey!' said Bruiser. 'Tha's a new one. What time do yer want me?'

'Tilly's fixed up a meeting at Catberry Manor at two tomorrow so when do you think we should leave?'

''Bout one-thirty should do it. I'll bring Miss Scarlet round ta the front of the bakery then. It's out past Wither-Fork Hall so it shouldn't take us more than 'arf an hour as long as them roads aren't flooded.'

'Perfect,' said Hettie, preparing to make a dash for it as the rain beat down on Bruiser's shed roof.

In spite of her mac, she was soaked to the skin by the time she returned to Tilly. Kicking off her wellingtons and leaving her mac in the puddle it had made by the door, she grabbed her dressing gown, pulling it round her she settled into her chair by the fire to dry off while Tilly made the tea and served the supper.

The pies were good and the *Tom and Jerry* cartoons mildly amusing, but Hettie and Tilly's thoughts had turned to the prospect of a new case, both pleased that at last they had something to get their teeth into – and fascinated by the possibility of death by chocolate.

Chapter Two

It was the rain beating on the windowpanes that woke Tilly from a deep sleep rather than the Butter sisters' bread ovens, which were situated in the hall outside their bedsitter. Betty and Beryl usually fired up their ovens at around four-thirty each morning but today was different. Tilly rubbed her eyes and looked across at her Top Cat alarm clock, realising that she had overslept. It was ten minutes to nine. She leapt out of her fleecy blanket and pulled the door open as Betty approached from the bakery with a tray in her paws, offering a full vocal performance of 'It Might As Well Rain Until September'.

'I thought something was wrong when I didn't hear the ovens this morning,' said Tilly, taking the laden tray of frothy coffees and bacon baps that Betty proffered.

'Bless you,' said Betty, 'we've been baking less but we've still got plenty of bread and pies from yesterday's bake, so we've filled the shelves with those in hopes that folk will dodge the raindrops. We've had no breakfast trade this morning so Sister has filled a couple of baps with bacon for you and Hettie before it goes off. It's a case of eat-up and we're relying on you two and Bruiser to help us out. There'll be filled crusty cobs for your lunch and at least two pies each for your supper and I've no idea what we're supposed to do with a whole batch of cream horns. We've enough to start an orchestra.'

'I'm very happy to help with those, as you know they're my favourite,' said Tilly, 'but what will you do if the rain doesn't stop and no one comes to buy anything?'

'Well, as our old mother used to say, you can't eat toast without making crumbs. I think she was being optimistic but I'm not entirely sure.'

Tilly looked a little puzzled at Betty's pearl of Lancashire wisdom but decided to change the subject before things got even more complicated. 'We think we've got a new case out at Catberrys chocolate factory so we're going there this afternoon.'

'Well I never!' said Betty. 'You two certainly move in high circles – that family is almost royalty. Old Mr Catberry used to get his chauffeur to stop outside the bakery so he could buy one of Beryl's egg custards. He told us that he was sick of eating things covered in chocolate and that a custard tart was his idea of heaven. He made us promise not to tell old Mrs Catberry if we saw her. The funny thing was that she used to come in and secretly buy one of my Battenbergs and eat the whole thing in the car before she got back to Catberry Manor. I think she felt the same way about chocolate but it made them millionaires several times over. Shame about the chocolate Mog Nob, though – not a nice way to go. They say she's become a recluse since old Mr Catberry died. Mind you, there's plenty of space to rattle around in in that big old mansion they've got out there. Proper spooky, by all accounts.'

'Why? Is it haunted?' asked Tilly, keen to glean as much information as she could.

'I'm not sure exactly but rumour has it that there are plenty of skeletons in their cupboards. You'd expect that in a family like the Catberrys, though. Anyway, you enjoy your breakfast. Sister and me will look forward to hearing about your Catberry experience later. I'd better get back in case we have a customer.'

Betty returned to the bakery and Tilly delivered the breakfast tray to the table before attempting to wake Hettie. It was never an easy task, but since moving in to share their small bedsitter, it was something that Tilly had happily taken on. She approached Hettie's chair and gently informed the heaped-up tangle of dressing gown and long-haired tabby fur that there was a bacon bap and a frothy coffee available. The bundle gradually began to stir as two paws reached out and stretched, followed by a head with twitching whiskers.

Hettie rubbed her eyes and proceeded to lick her paws and wash her face as Tilly fetched a bacon bap and one of the coffees from the table, placing them on the arm of Hettie's chair before collecting her own breakfast and settling down with it on her fleecy blanket.

The two cats chewed enthusiastically on the generous pile of bacon that Beryl had forced into the baps, barely pausing to wash it down with the frothy coffee until there was nothing left but a few stray crumbs. 'That was probably the best bacon bap I've ever had,' said Hettie, leaning back in her chair and wiping froth from her mouth with the back of her paw. 'I couldn't eat another thing until lunchtime.'

'We've got filled crusty cobs coming for lunch and double pies for supper,' said Tilly, as she picked some bacon out of her teeth with one of her claws. 'I'm getting a bit worried about the bakery and the lack of customers. Betty and Beryl didn't even have the ovens on this morning, as they had too many leftovers from yesterday.'

'I'm sure things will pick up as soon as it stops raining. The store cupboards around the town must be running on empty by now and no cat is going to starve itself when it doesn't have to. With the weekend coming, I think things will pick up. Looking on the bright side, it's a win-win situation for us and we're helping out by eating up all the stuff that isn't sold.'

Tilly didn't entirely agree with Hettie's reasoning but was keen to update her on Betty's conversation regarding the Catberry family.

'Skeletons in cupboards, you say? I wonder if they're covered in chocolate like the ones in the vat?' pondered Hettie. 'I think this may turn out to be a very interesting case. Did Betty say anything about Pettifur Catberry? I assume he's the son of old Mr Catberry?'

Tilly shook her head. 'No, she didn't mention him, but he did sound really posh on the phone – a bit clipped, like he was used to giving orders, if you know what I mean.'

'Running a huge business like Catberrys, I suppose you have to be a bit dictatorial. Having tons of money must make a difference to how you behave and you can eat as much chocolate as you like for free.'

'I thought I might see if the Catberrys are mentioned in my *Who's What* book before we go,' said Tilly, 'but I haven't seen it for ages.'

'It's underneath the sideboard, right at the back with your green shield stamp books,' said Hettie. 'Isn't it about time you cashed them in for something nice?'

'I'm saving them up for a new leather biker's jacket for Bruiser's birthday, as he gets me most of the stamps when he fills Miss Scarlet up with petrol,' said Tilly, crawling under the sideboard and emerging covered in cobwebs and clutching her *Who's What*. 'It's a secret, which is why I keep them hidden. I need another whole book before I can get the jacket from the catalogue.'

The rain was now lashing against the window. Hettie pulled her dressing gown closer to her and put some sticks and rolled-up newspaper in the fireplace, adding some small lumps of coal; soon there was a cheery blaze to warm the room.

Tilly, having sneezed away the cobwebs, settled down again on her blanket to paw through her book, looking for the Catberrys. She wasn't disappointed. 'There's a whole two pages on them and a family tree that's really impressive, starting with the original Catberry brothers. It says here that they started by selling chocolate drinks to encourage cats to stop drinking gin in late Victorian times. They were called Hauxston and Solomon Catberry.'

'Do-gooders and spoilsports, then,' suggested Hettie, as Tilly read on.

'Hauxston and Solomon built a factory to give poor cats jobs and started making chocolates to sell to rich cats. They became so successful that they had to move to bigger premises so they bought a load of land and built a larger factory, a mansion house and a village for the workers to live in, which is known today as Catberry-on-the-Brink because the river Brink runs through the land and is used as a water supply for the chocolate.'

'Fascinating,' said Hettie, rather sarcastically. 'Nothing like chaining your workers' noses to the grindstone.'

'I think that's a bit unfair,' said Tilly. 'It says that the brothers really cared about their workers and gave them holidays at the seaside and good rates of pay until the factory burnt down.'

'Now it's getting interesting! Then what happened?'

Tilly scanned the next paragraph before commenting. 'Oh dear, according to this the brothers fell out over the fire. Hauxston accused Solomon of leaving one of his cigars burning in the packing area. Solomon denied starting the fire and left his brother to seek his fortune in America, where he started a rival chocolate and bubblegum factory called Solomon's Candy Clump. Hauxston was left to rebuild the Catberry factory with the help of his two sons, Joshua and Sylvester.'

'And they all lived happily ever after?' suggested Hettie.

Tilly shook her head. 'No, it just gets worse. On the day the new factory opened, Hauxston had a platform built outside the factory to celebrate so that he could address the workers. He was so overexcited that he fell off the stage and was trampled to death by the marching band he'd booked for the occasion.'

'I'm trying really hard to keep a straight face,' said Hettie. 'What happened next?'

'According to this, Joshua and Sylvester made a real go of things, business boomed and they branched out into biscuits as well as chocolates, inventing lots of new lines until the epidemic.'

'I'm on the edge of my seat now. This is better than anything on the TV.'

'I'm surprised they haven't made it into one of those biopics, like the one we watched on Elizabeth

Traybake,' said Tilly, keen to use the word 'biopic' as she'd only just learnt it from the entertainment section of the *Daily Snout*.

'Never mind your posh words – what epidemic?' asked Hettie. 'You can't just leave me dangling.'

'It says that Horace Catberry, son of Sylvester, caught cat flu at his boarding school and was sent home. He managed to infect some of the workers and it spread throughout the factory, killing half the workforce, including his Uncle Joshua. The factory had to be closed as they didn't have enough cats to make the chocolates. It was known as the Great Flu of Forty-One. Sylvester worked hard to get the factory up and running again by introducing machinery to replace the workers who'd died and that's when they stopped making paw-made chocolates. Sylvester Catberry was the first factory owner to have a conveyor belt, evidently. He used to ride on it at the beginning of each day to say good morning to his workers.'

'Until?' suggested Hettie. 'I feel another disaster threatening the house of Catberry.'

Tilly shook her head. 'No, from then on everything seemed to run smoothly along with the chocolate. According to these dates, Sylvester made very old bones and was succeeded by Horace, who we know as old Mr Catberry – the one who died recently, leaving his widow Praline, his son Pettifur and two daughters, Lolly and Rhubarb. Rhubarb married the factory manager, Oliver Crumbwell. Lolly doesn't seem to have married anyone as yet but that's all there is unless Pettifur has married and had kittens.'

'Just a minute,' said Hettie. 'You said that Rhubarb Catberry married Oliver Crumbwell so doesn't that make her Rhubarb Crumbwell?'

It took quite some time for the two cats to stop giggling.

Chapter Three

Bruiser was good to his word and was waiting with Miss Scarlet at the front of the bakery. The three cats had enjoyed a crusty cob lunch from the Butters' surplus stock and were now ready to face the prospect of Catberry Manor and all that it might entail. The rain had stopped long enough for several cats to venture into the bakery and Tilly was greatly relieved to see them leaving with shopping bags overflowing with the Butter sisters' pies and pastries. Even the tray of cream horns had been dented, but she was pleased to note that Beryl had put two aside, along with a large chicken and ham plate pie and two pasties for hers and Hettie's supper. Bruiser's reward for braving the rain to collect a multitude of snails and slugs from Betty and Beryl's flower borders and pots was a large paper bag containing two of his favourite beef and onion pies and a generous slice of apple sponge traybake. With their suppers secured, Hettie and Tilly jumped into the sidecar and were about to give Bruiser the nod to be on their way when Beryl came bustling out of the bakery.

'Just a minute,' she said, waving a paper bag at them. 'As you're going out to the factory, you can take this for old Mrs Catberry. It's one of Sister's Battenbergs – we've got a tray of them without homes at the moment.'

Hettie passed the bag to Tilly, who put it into her satchel. Securing the lid on the sidecar, Bruiser kicked the motorbike into life and headed down the high street, avoiding as many puddles as possible.

The countryside, like the town, looked drenched, with many of the fields turned to lakes where trees barely lifted the top of their branches out of the water. Ducks, geese and swans seemed to be the only creatures pleased with the wet weather, expanding their domains far beyond the rivers and streams to which they were accustomed. The roads were just about passable, with the ditches on either side overflowing. Bruiser expertly avoided areas of deep water but was relieved to see the giant chimneys of the chocolate factory in the distance and the Gothic turrets of Catberry Manor. In a matter of minutes, he entered the village of Catberry-on-the-Brink and swung the motorbike off the main road on to a long rhododendron-lined driveway leading to the manor. At the end of the drive there was parking for several cars and Bruiser pulled up next to an impressive Rolls-Royce.

'That's quite some house,' said Hettie, wiping the condensation off the sidecar window. 'It reminds me a bit of Count Catula's castle.'

Tilly shivered. 'I hate that film. He was a nasty piece of work – those bloodshot eyes and horrible fangs gave me nightmares for weeks.'

'Let's just hope that the resemblance stops at the creepy house in front of us and that Pettifur Catberry prefers drinking chocolate to blood,' said Hettie, pushing the lid back on the sidecar. 'Come on – we don't want to keep our new client waiting.'

Hettie leapt out onto the gravel and straightened her mac, which was still damp from the night before. Tilly followed a little less enthusiastically, leaving Bruiser to settle himself down in the sidecar out of the rain with the latest edition of *Bikers' Monthly*. The two cats climbed several steps to an impressive front door with a highly polished brass knocker and a bell pull to one side. Hettie pulled on it and instantly heard it ring out into the depths of the house. There was no immediate response and she was about to pull it again when the door creaked open on hinges begging to be oiled, revealing a cat dressed in a chocolate-and-yellow-coloured livery.

'Good afternoon,' said Hettie. 'We are from The No. 2 Feline Detective Agency and we have an appointment with Mr Pettifur Catberry.'

'Very good,' said the cat. 'If you'd like to step this way, Mr Catberry will see you in the day room.' The cat wrenched Hettie and Tilly's macs off them, looking them up and down as if he were inspecting their suitability for meeting his master, which reminded

Tilly even more of the *Catula* film. The dark panelled hallway leading to the biggest sweeping staircase she'd ever seen didn't ease her feeling of foreboding. She clung to her satchel, fearing that it was also going to be wrestled from her and followed the servant, sticking very close to Hettie.

To her surprise and relief, Pettifur Catberry was nothing like the vampire cat. The servant showed them into a light and attractive room full of rather lovely things, announcing to his master the arrival of Hettie Bagshot and Tilly Jenkins.

The Catberrys were clearly collectors: there was a display of gaily painted pottery, some beautiful silver snuffboxes and a gallery of landscape scenes adorned the walls. Their host stood by a roaring fire, a cat who undoubtedly enjoyed his food and had a jolly look about him. He was short and suited the rather loud yellow-checked waistcoat and matching jacket that he wore; his breeches were tucked into a pair of bright red socks, set off to perfection by shining buckled shoes. The round spectacles on the end of his nose made him look intelligent but not unapproachable. Tilly instantly thought of a picture she'd seen of Mr Pickwick, but settled on Toad of Toad Hall as a closer resemblance.

'Welcome to Catberry Manor,' he said in the same clipped voice that Tilly had heard on the telephone. 'I trust your journey wasn't too hampered by the weather?'

Hettie shook her head. 'No, we managed to avoid the floods.'

'It occurred to me that I should have sent a car under the circumstances but I'm pleased you were able to respond so quickly to my request for a meeting. Please, sit down.' Pettifur signalled to two comfortable chairs close to the fire and settled himself into a high-backed carver chair, that instantly gave him an air of authority. 'I gather from some of the things I've read about you both that you are very successful in your profession. Your reputation goes before you. The fact is I'm deeply concerned about the damage that the discovery of bodies in one of my chocolate vats will do to my business. I trust I can rely on you both to be discreet in your investigations?'

'Of course,' said Hettie. 'Perhaps you'd like to start from the beginning? When were the bodies discovered?'

'Well, it came to my attention yesterday afternoon. My brother-in-law is the factory manager here and oversees everything. Oliver is married to my youngest sister Rhubarb, who runs the biscuit section, and I very much regard him as family. We've been updating some of the equipment and machinery recently, which includes several of the older chocolate vats. We took delivery of the new ones last week and I'm pleased to say they're up and running with no break in production. The old vats were moved to our packing warehouse to be cleaned and sent for scrap and it was while one of them was being hosed out that Oliver made the grim discovery.'

'And what exactly did he find?' prompted Hettie, as Tilly reached into her satchel for her notepad and pencil and found herself a clean page.

'At first he wasn't too sure. He thought that the residues at the bottom of the vat were lumps of hardened chocolate but on closer inspection he realised that there were bones sticking up and he called me immediately. I cast my eye across it and called you. My wife Morgana reads a lot of these dreadful crime books and said we should leave everything untouched until you arrived to view the situation so we've cordoned off the area ready for your inspection.'

'Excellent,' said Hettie. 'Perhaps we should take a look now so that we can see what we're dealing with.'

'Yes, of course. I'll get Oliver to come over and take you to the factory,' said Pettifur, rising and reaching for the telephone on a table by the door. The call was picked up instantly. 'Oliver, the detectives are here and would like to see the chocolate vat. If you'd be kind enough to fetch Miss Bagshot and Miss Jenkins now?'

Satisfied with the response, Pettifur replaced the receiver. 'He'll be here in a couple of minutes. Perhaps you'd like to join Morgana and me for tea when you've finished so we can discuss a way forward?'

At the mention of tea, Tilly suddenly remembered the Battenberg cake Beryl had given her and felt for it in her satchel. 'Before we go over to the factory, could

I leave this with you?' she asked rather timidly, handing it to Pettifur. 'Betty and Beryl from the bakery in the town have sent it for your mother.'

He looked a little confused until he stared into the bag, then he smiled. 'How very kind of them,' he said. 'I'm afraid she rarely stirs from her rooms since my father's death but I'll see she gets it. I'm sure it will brighten her day.'

There was a polite knock at the door and the servant entered. 'Mr Oliver is here to take your visitors over to the factory. Shall I show them to the door?'

'Thank you, Sparks, and we'll take tea with my guests at four.'

Sparks nodded and Hettie and Tilly followed him out of the day room and back to the front door. The servant retrieved their macs from the hall stand and held them out at arm's length for Hettie and Tilly to put on. He then pulled the front door open to reveal a torrential downpour and a giant Creamy Egg on wheels, parked on the gravel with its engine running. The cat driving it leapt out and pushed the passenger seat forward to allow Tilly to clamber into the back then slid it back again for Hettie to get in and jumped in beside her.

Oliver Crumbwell introduced himself, then sped off down the driveway and back on to the main road, taking the next turning up to the chocolate factory. The drive was all too short for Tilly, who was utterly captivated by the chocolate brown, yellow and white vehicle they were travelling in. Oliver brought the Creamy Egg to a standstill next to a whole fleet of similar vehicles, all bearing the famous distinctive colour branding that appeared on Catberrys products. The factory complex was impressive and boasted several buildings the size of aircraft hangers – some with tall chimneys trailing smoke – and a single-storey office block and staff canteen.

'We're heading for that building over there,' said Oliver. 'It doesn't look like this rain is going to stop so we'd better make a run for it.' The cat opened the door and moved swiftly round to the passenger side to let Hettie out, pushing the seat forward for Tilly to escape. The three cats splashed their way towards the building that Oliver had indicated and in through the door to a giant loading bay, piled to the ceiling with pallets of chocolates and biscuits ready to make their way to shops across the country. A large van, painted in the same colours as everything else, was being loaded by a cat driving a forklift truck. Another female cat stood by the van with a clipboard, counting the boxes as they were skilfully pushed into the vehicle.

'This way, 'said Oliver. 'The vat you need to see is at the other end of the loading bay, where we do our repairs and maintenance.'

Hettie and Tilly followed Oliver to an area where four giant vats stood. The section had been roped off, with a sign saying 'Danger. Keep Out'. 'This is where we found them. If you climb up the ladder, you can see for yourself.'

Oliver pointed his paw to the ladder fixed to the side of the vat and Hettie wasted no time in climbing it, leaving Tilly to watch. The vat was at least ten times taller than she was and once she reached the top and leaned over, there was no doubt what she was looking at. The first thought that came into her mind was a mud fight suspended in time. The hardened chocolate had set around the shapes at the bottom of the container and had it not been for the bones sticking out, the bodies might have gone undetected and could easily have made their way to the scrapyard to be crushed along with any normal load of unwanted metal. Several questions sprang instantly to Hettie's mind. When had they been put into the vat? And how many bodies were there in the mass of hardened chocolate? She climbed carefully back down the ladder, pleased to be on firm ground again.

'How long has the vat been here?' she asked, as Tilly pulled her notepad and pencil out of her satchel.

'We changed the vats over last week but I only got round to hosing them down yesterday,' said Oliver. 'I've arranged for them to be taken to the scrapyard at the end of this week, as we need them out of the way.'

'What about these other vats?'

'All as clean as a whistle, hosed down and ready to go. It was just The Tabby in Black and I stopped hosing it down as soon as I saw the bones sticking out.'

'What do you mean by The Tabby in Black? Do the vats have names?'

Oliver shook his head. 'No, but the chocolate does. This vat was used for the dark chocolate that goes into The Tabby in Black selection boxes. That one was for Fruit and Nip, the one in front of it was for Creamy Eggs and that one over there was for The Furry Milk selection. We have to be careful not to mix them up and we can't have any contamination because all our chocolates have their own unique flavours. Some of the receipts go back as far as Sylvester Catberry's time. He actually invented The Tabby in Black range – it's one of our bestsellers – and he took the business into biscuits too.'

'And Pettifur Catberry is his grandson?'

'Yes, that's right. My wife Rhubarb is Sylvester's granddaughter. She inherited the biscuit section when her father died last month, although she's always been involved in the biscuits.'

'Do other members of the family work here?' asked Hettie.

'Most of them, although some have retired now. Rhubarb's mother Praline hasn't been the same since Horace died. In her day she created all the fillings for our various assortments; now she has no real interest in the business but is still very much head of the family. Lolly, Rhubarb's sister, has become her carer, although she used to do the wages in the office and arrange our open days, but now she looks after Praline full time, not that she needs much looking after. Pettifur has twin daughters with his late wife Caramela, Dandy and Grace. Grace is in charge of quality control and Dandy looks after the seasonal lines for Easter, Christmas and Valentine's Day. She's just introduced a Halloween range, which we'll be launching later this year. Right up her street, really, as she's a Goth and has a girl band with Grace and two other workers here. They go out as Gums and Noses – you may have heard of them. That's Crusty Catsick over there with the clipboard, although I'm sure that isn't her real name. She plays bass in the band and the cat on the forklift is their manager cum roadie. He calls himself Johnny Clash for professional reasons.'

'Having a band is quite a commitment,' observed Hettie, 'especially if you have a full-time job as well.'

'Horace was very keen on the workers in the factory having outside interests and he supported them, just like his father before him. As well as Grace and Dandy's band, we have our own theatre group, football and cricket teams, a retirement home, and – until recently – a darts team.'

'What happened to that?' asked Hettie, getting far too involved in the day-to-day lives of the chocolate workers.

'Pettifur decided that it was becoming too violent. The final straw was when we played the McKitties jam and shortbread factory just before Christmas. Four players were injured by darts and three others were caught fighting in the car park of the Mop and Bucket, out at Much-Purring-on-the-Rug. One of our players is still on sick leave, which has left us short on the dip and drop machine.'

It was clear to Hettie that Oliver Crumbwell cared a great deal for his job and all the responsibility that came with it and, as the case progressed, she would be pleased to know that there would be at least one cat she could rely on to fill her in on the intricacies of a family-run business, but just now all her attention was on the contents of The Tabby in Black container. 'Whatever is at the bottom of that vat will need a closer look,' she said, moving the conversation back to the case in paw. 'I'd like to put a call in to Shroud and Trestle, the undertakers in the town. Morbid Balm, their mortician, often helps us with bodies found in suspicious circumstances. She's very good on causes of death and I'd like her to collect the remains of who-ever or whatever is in that vat and take a closer look at what we have here.'

Oliver nodded in agreement. 'I'll drive you back to the Manor and you can call her from there. I'll be pleased to have the problem off the premises, to be honest. I'm not used to finding bodies in the chocolate.'

Hettie felt that was a bit of an understatement but she said nothing. Tilly put her notepad and pencil back into her satchel and the three cats returned to the Creamy Egg car. The rain had stopped briefly but there was flooding in the car park and Oliver drove very slowly back to Catberry Manor, taking care to avoid the deeper areas of water.

'I will need to speak to you again,' said Hettie, getting out of the car and pushing the seat forward for Tilly, 'but I think it would be a good idea to get Morbid Balm's thoughts on the bodies first. Thank you for your help this afternoon and your insights into the family.'

'It was a pleasure to meet you both and I'll help in any way I can. I'll make sure Miss Balm can retrieve the bodies when she arrives. I think the best way is to lay the vat on its side so she'll be able to walk straight in. I'll go back and get Johnny to help me with that now.'

They waved Oliver off and walked across to Miss Scarlet, where Bruiser was enjoying a sandwich and a cup of tea in the sidecar. 'I see they're looking after you,' Hettie said, as Bruiser slid back the lid and grinned.

'This is me third sandwich and me second cup o' tea – an' I've got a huge slice of chocolate cake ta finish off. A pretty little cat from the kitchins keeps bringin' me things. I think I'm goin' ta like this job.'

'It's certainly going to be different, that's for sure,' said Hettie. 'We're invited for afternoon tea but we shouldn't be long. I'm going to get Morbid to pick up the bodies and we should know more after that.'

'Right'o,' said Bruiser, closing the lid and getting back to his sandwich.

Hettie and Tilly made their way up the steps to the front door. Having seen them arrive, Sparks was waiting to divest them of their macs and show them back into the day room, where afternoon tea was about to be served.

Chapter Four

With Pettifur's permission, Hettie put in a call to Shroud and Trestle and was lucky to have it answered by Morbid herself. The Goth cat loved her profession and was very good at it, making it a personal mission to send all the cats in her care to their graves looking the very best they could. Her talents were immeasurable but she particularly enjoyed helping Hettie and Tilly out on their cases, which invariably included murder victims – a far cry from the day-to-day business of a small town undertaker, where most clients died of flu or old age. Hettie explained the situation and Morbid sounded excited at the prospect of chocolate corpses, offering to collect them in her van within the hour.

Pleased to get the investigation underway, Hettie and Tilly settled to an afternoon tea with Pettifur and Morgana Catberry. Morgana entered the room at the precise moment that the tea was being poured into china cups by a young female cat who bobbed a curtsey as her mistress arrived. Morgana glided across to one of the chairs by the fire as if she were walking on air. She was tall and very beautiful and everything about her screamed expensive: her painted claws dripped with rings and the delicate ballet shoes that peeped out from under her long flowing dress were studded with tiny jewels that sparkled as she walked.

Tilly was mesmerised by her but Hettie's attention was drawn to the tea laid out before them as Pettifur prepared to make the introductions. 'My dear, this is Miss Hettie Bagshot and Miss Tilly Jenkins from the detective agency I told you about. They've come to sort out the problem that Oliver discovered yesterday.'

Morgana looked Hettie and Tilly up and down before reaching for an iced bun. She began to nibble on it, taking care not to smudge the bright red lipstick that accentuated her rather thin lips. At that moment, Hettie decided to take an instant dislike to Morgana Catberry and Tilly wished that she'd joined Bruiser in the sidecar to share his chocolate cake.

Pettifur seemed oblivious to his wife's rudeness, signalling for Hettie and Tilly to sit on one of the sofas while the maid served them tea, putting a cake stand laden with tiny sandwiches and buns on a small table in front of them. 'Do help yourselves,' he said. 'I'm keen to have your thoughts on your visit to the factory. I hope Oliver was helpful?'

Normally Hettie and Tilly would have demolished the high tea in front of them but the atmosphere in the day room had become quite uncomfortable with the arrival of Morgana, who sat watching their every move. Both cats decided that they weren't in the slightest bit hungry. Tilly politely sipped her tea, which was much too strong for her, as Hettie made a gallant attempt at conversation with Pettifur who had remained standing. 'Yes, Oliver was very helpful. He gave us an overview of the factory and your family connections with it. It's quite a dynasty you have here and it's good to see that each generation has been happy to take it on.'

'Take it on!' snapped Morgana, tossing the half-eaten bun back onto her plate. 'You have no idea what it's like to live in this family with such a rope around our necks. Every waking moment is about that factory and the cats who work there. Chocolate this and biscuit that, bowing and scraping to the memory of long-dead Catberrys. It's a pity they're not all at the bottom of the chocolate vat rather than taking up spaces in the family mausoleum. Even the walls in there are brown and yellow.'

Pettifur hopped from one foot to another with embarrassment at Morgana's outburst. He was about to try and smooth things over but she stood up and flounced out of the room, pushing the maid out of her way as she went.

'I'm so terribly sorry about that,' Pettifur said, dismissing the maid with a wave of his paw. 'Morgana is still in shock after my father's death and she's only just coming to terms with my inheritance and my new responsibilities. My first wife Caramela died a couple of years ago so Morgana and I are virtually newly-weds. I fear that she didn't know what she was letting herself in for and this business with the bodies in the vat hasn't helped. It's rather thrown us all, to be honest.'

Now that Morgana had left the room, Hettie's appetite returned and she reached for a sandwich. Tilly abandoned her strong tea and did the same. 'I'm very sorry to hear about your first wife,' said Hettie. 'Was she more interested in the business than Morgana?'

'Absolutely,' said Pettifur finally picking up his own cup of tea, 'and the family loved her. She had time for everyone and raised our two beautiful daughters, Dandy and Grace. She was looking forward to the day when I would inherit from my father but sadly it wasn't to happen in her lifetime.'

Tilly, who'd just enjoyed two salmon sandwiches, couldn't resist a question of her own. 'What happened to her?'

'A tragic accident at the factory,' said Pettifur. 'She'd gone across to collect some samples to try from The Furry Milk selection and she didn't come back. I went to see what was keeping her and found her lying dead under a pallet of Catnip bars in the packing department. It must have toppled onto her when she was looking for the samples.'

Hettie was a little surprised by how easily Pettifur passed off his first wife's death as an accident but put her feelings down to the suspicious nature which often served her well as a detective. She did, however, find it curious that Oliver Crumbwell hadn't mentioned Caramela's accidental death during his detailed appraisal of the family but time was ticking on and there was really nothing more to discuss until Morbid had done her work. 'If you'll excuse us, I think we should be getting back to the town,' she said. 'I'm hoping that Morbid Balm will contact us tomorrow and, depending on her findings, we will draw up a plan for our investigations. I assume that you'll be happy for us to talk to members of the family and workforce if necessary?'

'Of course,' said Pettifur, 'and I'll see you out myself.'

The cat put his empty cup and saucer on the mantelpiece and crossed to the door. Hettie and Tilly followed him down the hall, where Sparks seemed to have appeared from nowhere to help them on with their macs.

'Until tomorrow, then?' said Pettifur, before turning on his heel and retracing his steps towards the day room.

Seeing Hettie and Tilly emerge from the Manor, Bruiser leapt out of the sidecar and started the motorbike. Hettie clambered in first, followed by Tilly, who pulled the lid shut to avoid getting any wetter in the rain.

Morgana Catberry watched from one of the many upstairs windows. As the detectives drove away, she turned back into the room and threw the book she'd been reading at the mirror over the fireplace. A scream of anger and frustration rose in her throat but the house was so big that nobody heard her.

Chapter Five

Hettie and Tilly were pleased to get home. The journey back to the town had been quite perilous and Bruiser had had to take a considerable detour to avoid the now severely flooded areas that had been passable earlier in the day.

'I hope Morbid got through the floods all right,' said Tilly, abandoning her wet mac on top of Hettie's on the doormat and crossing to the kettle, desperate for a proper milky tea, 'and I hope she'll be able to help us with the chocolate bodies.'

'I'm surprised that Oliver Crumbwell hasn't suggested they market them as a new line,' said Hettie, as she laid the fire and put a match to it. 'The Catberrys seem to have their claws in so many pies and it's all sewn up within the family. That place must be a goldmine. Pettifur seems to be a safe pair of paws to run the business but I can't wait to meet the rest of them if Morgana is anything to go by. She clearly hates Catberrys with a passion. I wouldn't be at all surprised if she hadn't tipped a few bodies into the chocolate to scupper the whole operation.'

'I thought she was going to be lovely when she came into that room,' said Tilly. 'She really is quite beautiful – more like a film star. I'm not sure that she and Pettifur are much of a match though. I wonder how they got together?'

'I suspect she was in it more for the money than the chocolate, judging by the way she was dressed – a real lady of the manor, dripping with jewels supplied by a husband who dotes on her. I suppose old Horace Catberry's premature death took her by surprise. Now she's the boss's wife, trapped in a family she's hardly got to know.'

'I wonder what her two stepdaughters think of her?' said Tilly. 'I can't see her attending many of their Gums and Noses gigs. And what about old Mrs Catberry, her mother-in-law? How do they get on?'

'Well, I can't see them sharing a Battenberg, that's for sure,' said Hettie, warming her paws on the fire, 'and judging by what we witnessed today, I think Pettifur may have to look for another wife to share his chocolates with. I do find the whole idea of a family empire fascinating though. This may turn out to be a really interesting case for us.'

'I'd better go and hang our macs over the bread ovens before supper,' said Tilly. 'We'll need them tomorrow and they're both wet through. I'll make the tea when I get back.'

She stepped out into the back hallway just as Betty and Beryl descended the stairs from their flat above the bakery. 'We thought we heard you come in,' said Betty. 'How did you get on with the Catberrys?'

'We only met a couple of them,' said Tilly, draping the macs over the bread ovens, 'and Oliver Crumbwell, who's married to Rhubarb, Pettifur's sister. We had tea with Pettifur, who inherited the factory from old Mr Catberry, and Morgana was there too. He seems quite nice but Morgana was really rude about the chocolate business.'

'That doesn't surprise me,' said Beryl. 'Morgana Cutlet, as was, fortune hunter and femme fatale to any cat stupid enough to take her on.'

'That Pettifur Catberry wasn't the first of her conquests either,' added Betty. 'She tried her luck with the heir to McKitties biscuits before she got her claws into chocolate. He was sensible enough to see how that cookie crumbled before it was too late though.'

Hettie, who'd been listening with interest through the open door, joined them in the hallway. 'How do you know all this?'

'Ah well, that's down to Walter, who delivers to us,' said Beryl. 'He works for McKitties, so he picks up all the confectionery gossip that's going. According to Walter, McKitties and Catberrys have been arch rivals since Catberrys went into biscuits and McKitties started covering their digestives in chocolate. A war of crumbs rather than words, I suppose you could say, but Morgana Cutlet just made things worse.'

'In what way?' asked Hettie, intrigued by Morgana's past aspirations.

'She played one off against the other, making out that she was the catch of the century. Poor old Pettifur fell for it hook, line and sinker, showering gifts on her, taking her for posh holidays and promising her the earth. Their photos were all over *Vanity Hair*. They had one of those big society weddings and a whole month on honeymoon. I bet Morgana came down from all of that with a crash when she had to settle into Catberry Manor. "Marry in haste and live on fish paste", as our mother would say if she was here now.'

Betty nodded sagely at her sister's words, before pulling the subject back to the goings-on at Catberry Manor. 'So what's happened out there to make them call you two in?' she asked.

'They've found what they think are bodies in one of their vats of chocolate,' said Hettie.

Silenced momentarily by the revelation, the two sisters looked at each other and shook their heads before Betty found her tongue. 'Well, that beggars belief. I won't be buying you any more boxes of Furry Milk, Sister, that's for sure – not now we know what might be in them.'

'I think that's a major concern of Pettifur's,' said Hettie. 'I hope we don't need to ask but please keep that to yourselves. If it gets out that there are bodies in their chocolate it will most certainly be the end of Catberrys.'

'As always, our lips are sealed,' said Betty. 'Come on, Sister – *Top of the Pots* is about to start, that new gardening show with Minty Dumb. Then it's early to bed, as we've baking to do first thing.'

The Butter sisters retreated to their flat and Hettie and Tilly settled by their fire to watch TV and enjoy their supper, knowing that tomorrow would bring a visit to Shroud and Trestle, the town's undertakers.

Chapter Six

Tilly was greatly relieved to hear the bread ovens being fired up, even though it was four-thirty in the morning. She pulled her fleecy blanket over her head and went back to sleep, contented to know that the Butter sisters were hopeful of customers in spite of the rain. Friday and Saturday were normally busy times in the high street, as the cats of the town shopped, gossiped and associated with friends in Molly Bloom's café. The rain had lasted for weeks, but as the spring flowers had begun to appear in gardens and hedgerows, there was a general feeling of hope for longer, sunnier days – and a need to be out and about, just as Hettie had predicted.

As there was a new case to investigate, Bruiser had decided to give Miss Scarlet a bit of an overhaul, as he put it; he was concerned about the amount of floodwater he'd had to drive her through on the way back from Catberry-on-the-Brink. When Hettie and Tilly finally woke up, Hettie opted to throw caution to the wind and walk to Shroud and Trestle to give Bruiser time to work on the motorbike, arranging to meet him for lunch at Bloomers later.

Having devoured several slices of cheese triangles on toast and three cups of milky tea each, Hettie and Tilly set out for Sheba Gardens, dressed in their newly dried-out macs and carrying Betty's large golfing umbrella. As they splashed down the high street, leaving a substantial queue behind them at the bakery where Betty and Beryl were almost up to full speed behind their counter, they were pleased that the rain had lapsed into a fine drizzle. As they passed Bloomers café, it was good to see it busy with cats enjoying Molly's all-day breakfasts and Malkin and Sprinkle's department store also seemed to be attracting quite a few customers to their extended winter sales. It would seem that the town was finally waking up from what had been an atrocious bout of wet weather, even though the forecast was still unreliable.

Shroud and Trestle was discreetly tucked away at the bottom of Sheba Gardens, a pleasant area of the town where many well-heeled cats lived. The undertaker's was a family business. Morbid Balm had joined them as a pall bearer, straight from school, and such was her enthusiasm and attention to detail that she'd very quickly become part of the firm, rising to the role of mortician and – when required – chief undertaker at particularly high-profile funerals. Black suited her as she was a Goth and prided herself on her piercings and decorative jewellery, much of which depicted her favourite occult symbols.

'I wonder what Morbid has found in the chocolate?' said Tilly, as they crossed the yard making their way into the reception area, where a pale and rather dowdy cat sat sporting a badge that announced her as Ethel Trestle.

Ethel offered a well-rehearsed, sympathetic, half-hearted smile to her visitors before launching into her professional patter. 'Welcome to Shroud and Trestle. We are a family-run undertakers who pride ourselves in offering help and support at this difficult time.'

Hettie raised her paw to stop the flow of condolences but Ethel pushed on regardless. 'We know and completely understand how you must be feeling at this terrible time, but rest assured – we will take you by the paw and lead you through the darkness, assuring you that your loved one will be safe in our care and offering a tailor-made service entirely fashioned to your requirements.'

Ethel took a breath and reached for a ring file on her desk. 'Mr Shroud will be with you shortly, but if you'd like to take a seat and peruse our brochure, I'm sure you'll find the perfect casket to lay your loved one to rest in. We also have a full range of colours should you require something special – our Day Glow collection of fluorescent pigments, perhaps, or the Aurora Glow in the Dark which has proved to be very popular with our younger clients.'

Ethel was about to launch into prospective burial grounds and crematoria when Morbid Balm came to the rescue through a door behind the reception desk. Hettie was almost disappointed that Ethel had been cut off in midstream, but Tilly was grateful as she was beginning to feel quite depressed about the subject matter. 'Thank you, Ethel,' said Morbid, lifting the flap next to the desk, 'but these are friends of mine come to talk about the chocolate corpses so they won't be needing a look at the brochure.'

Ethel seemed quite disappointed that she'd wasted her sales talk but cheered up instantly as another cat arrived looking tearful and sobbing into a handkerchief. Morbid beckoned Hettie and Tilly through to her preparation room, leaving Ethel to deal with the genuinely bereaved visitor.

The room where Morbid Balm performed her magic resembled an old-fashioned dairy. The walls were fully tiled from floor to ceiling; there was a large butler sink and several metal benches around the edge of the space, with one long metal table in the middle. The table had several skeletons laid out, all of which had been meticulously put back together.

'Not an easy one this,' she said, pointing her paw at the table. 'I had to heat the chocolate up with a blowtorch and a steaming kettle to retrieve the bones, which was a tricky business, and then I spent most of the night matching them up to make the skeletons.

There are three cats here and another one over there which is much more recently deceased.'

Morbid moved to one of the benches by the sink and lifted a sheet up to reveal a very dead cat that she had performed a post-mortem on. The corpse was virtually intact, with ginger fur and large staring eyes; its paws and whiskers still showed residues of chocolate. 'I can't speak for the skeletons, but this cat – who is female – was definitely dead before she went into the chocolate. There's no trace of chocolate in the lungs, you see, so she didn't drown.'

'So someone disposed of the body?' suggested Hettie. 'Do you have any idea how this cat died?'

'My guess is a bash on the head, as there were no other signs – but that could have happened when the body was dropped into the vat. She has a nasty cut across one of her paws, which occurred when she was alive and looks like it festered. This cat was quite old and might even have died of old age but she does have a fractured skull.'

Tilly was making frantic notes, trying very hard not to look at the dead cat, but Morbid hadn't quite finished with her findings. 'The skeletons have obviously lost all their flesh but I did recover their pelts from the chocolate as skin and fur take much longer to decompose. I washed the pelts and dried them. Judging by the size of the bones, we have one female and two male cats.'

Morbid crossed to a tall cabinet and opened the door to reveal the three pelts pegged up inside. 'We've got a short-haired female tabby, another ginger and a black one, both male, if that helps. I also found some bits and pieces of jewellery – an ear stud, a couple of rings, a broken pair of spectacles and an assortment of buttons from clothing. I found some strips of cloth but my guess is that these cats were virtually naked when they were put into the chocolate.'

'What about the skeletons?' Hettie asked, taking a closer look at them. 'Any idea how they might have died?'

Morbid returned to the table and shook her head. 'It's hard to say. Some of the bones have fractures and this one has a broken back, but that could easily have happened in the vat when they were tipped in. It would also depend on whether there was chocolate in the vat to cushion their fall, or if it was poured on them later, but the bones suggest that these cats were elderly too.'

Hettie returned to the ginger cat's body. 'You say this cat went into the vat more recently? Have you any idea how recently?'

'I'd hazard a guess at weeks but the chocolate might have acted as a preservative. If that's the case, those skeletons could be years old. There's no way of telling. I'd say you've got a right puzzle on your paws. Whoever is responsible has covered their tracks in chocolate.'

It was a rare thing for Morbid to joke about her work but her words lightened the mood a little, which

Tilly at least was grateful for. She loved being part of the detective agency, but working at the coalface when a body had to be viewed was something she found difficult, and Hettie did her best to protect her from the worst parts of the job. This time it was important that Tilly saw and understood the implications of the bodies in the chocolate, as she was in charge of noting down the details that might eventually lead to solving the case.

Morbid looked at her watch before covering up the ginger cat and the skeletons on the table. 'What do you want me to do with them?' she asked. 'We obviously can't arrange funerals until we know who they were but I could box up the skeletons and put the ginger cat in the freezer for now.'

'That would be kind,' said Hettie. 'I suppose Pettifur Catberry will have to decide once we know a bit more about them but at least we have one body that someone may be able to identify.'

Morbid nodded and pulled a small envelope out of a drawer in one of the benches. 'Maybe these personal effects might help too. Some of the jewellery looks quite valuable and the spectacles are almost antique – proper horn-rimmed. I'd say these cats probably had money.'

Tilly took the envelope from Morbid and put it in her satchel. 'We're meeting Bruiser for lunch at Bloomers,' said Hettie. 'You're welcome to join us if you have time?'

'I've got a removal at three but lunch sounds good,' said Morbid, divesting herself of her black mortician's apron and looking out of the window into the yard. 'I'll give you a lift to Bloomers in my van as it's chucking it down out there again. This weather isn't helping with the burials. The graves are filling up with water faster than we can get the coffins in them and the graveyard out at Much-Purring-on-the-Blanket is completely flooded. We'll have caskets floating down the roads if this rain keeps up.'

With that sombre thought well and truly planted in Hettie's and Tilly's minds, the three cats left the preparation room by the back door, not wishing to disturb Ethel Trestle and her new client, who was on her second box of complimentary tissues.

Chapter Seven

Although the journey from the undertakers to Bloomers was a short one, Hettie and Tilly were pleased to clamber out of Morbid's van and into the café. They were more than used to death in their investigations but there was something deeply depressing about a vehicle whose sole purpose was to collect and deliver under the saddest of circumstances.

Bloomers was buzzing with cats enjoying lunch as they swapped news and berated the awful weather that had kept them at home for so many weeks. There was a lot of catching up to do, so they lingered at their tables, and it was just as well that Molly had agreed to reserve a table permanently for The No. 2 Feline Detective Agency, tucked away at the back of the café, where Hettie and Tilly would often carry out interviews. It also helped that Bruiser was walking out with Dolly Scollop, a Cornish cat who ran the café with Molly. Molly's partnership with Dolly was a café made in heaven: the combination of Dolly's welcoming front-of-house skills and Molly's down-to-earth cookery was a winning tour de force in the high street.

Bruiser was waiting at their table as Hettie, Tilly and Morbid approached. The chatter that had hit them as they walked in had come to an abrupt halt at the sight of the Goth cat, not because she was a Goth but because she was an undertaker, well known to all in the town. It was something that Morbid had had to get used to in her early days at Shroud and Trestle; now she just smiled and nodded, doing her best to put everyone at ease.

Dolly was quick to attend to her new arrivals once they had settled into their chairs. 'We've got a selection of Butters' pies, liver and onions, and a proper Cornish pasty on the specials today,' she said, giving out the menus, 'an' we got cream mash or chips to go with 'em. For your puddin', there's a jam sponge with custard or ice cream, or a double treacle tart with almond crumb an' cream – Molly's been watchin' Delia Sniff's *Puddin's to Die For* on the telly.'

Dolly suddenly realised what she'd said, but Morbid offered her a smile, making it clear that no offence had been taken. The Cornish cat busied herself clearing tables while the four friends looked through the menu. Hettie, Tilly and Bruiser knew it off by heart but Morbid – who rarely had time for lunch – scrutinised it with great care.

Dolly returned to the table with her notepad and Tilly was the first to place her order. 'I'd like liver and onions with cream mash and some chips on the side to dip in the gravy and for pudding the treacle tart with cream.'

'And I'd like the liver with chips,' said Hettie, 'and the jam sponge for pudding with ice cream.'

Bruiser was still deciding but Morbid had made her mind up. 'I think I'll go for the fish and chips with mushy peas,' she said. 'I try to steer clear of meat as a rule, and banana custard would be lovely.'

Morbid's avoidance of meat hadn't been lost on Hettie, taking account of the job she did, but she said nothing and just raised her eyebrows at Tilly, who returned a knowing look. Bruiser had finally decided on the three-cheese omelette and chips, followed by rice pudding with chocolate crispies, and Dolly sped away to the kitchen where Molly was busy cooking and plating up.

Hettie brought Bruiser up to date with Morbid's findings and the Butters' revelations regarding Morgana, and Morbid listened with interest, eventually adding her own view of the Catberry family. 'We handled old Mr Catberry's funeral back in February,' she said. 'It was all a bit full-on, with Praline Catberry throwing herself on top of the coffin and giving it a good thumping with her paws once he'd been lowered into the ground. The whole of the family turned out for it, including Morgana, who was behaving like the spectre at the feast.'

'What do you mean?' asked Hettie.

'Well, you'd think it was her husband or father who'd died – she was so overdramatic and wailed constantly at the graveside. I almost thought she was being paid to do it. It was no wonder that Praline jumped into the grave just to get away from her. The worst of it was when they came to the undertakers to make the arrangements. Praline was clearly in shock after the Mog Nob accident and wouldn't let me lay him out properly. She wouldn't even agree to me removing the Mog Nob from his throat, but she brought a pile of papers with her to put in his coffin.'

'What sort of papers?'

'I thought they must have been love letters, as lots of them were tied with ribbon, but there were old documents too and a little notebook of paw-written recipes splashed with chocolate. As soon as I'd put them in the casket, she insisted I screw him down, leaving strict instructions not to let anyone view the body. Morgana came back later and asked to see him but I refused and she had an almighty tantrum which upset Ethel for days. The daughters – Lolly and Rhubarb – turned up later that week to pay their respects but I had to send them away as well, pointing out that their mother's wishes had to be respected.'

'It doesn't sound like normal behaviour for a bereaved family,' Hettie said.

'It's certainly up there with the difficult ones,' said Morbid, 'but arranging a funeral with a family like the Catberrys can be a nightmare, especially with a sudden death like Horace's. I gather he'd left no instructions for his funeral and his widow was in no mood to see the full picture. It was as if she wanted him in the ground as fast as possible without any thought for the rest of his family. We did try to persuade her to share the arrangements with Pettifur, Lolly and Rhubarb but she was having none of it.'

'What about the chocolate factory staff? Did they attend the funeral?'

'Absolutely. It was a massive turnout, even though it chucked it down. St Kipper's was packed to the rafters with family, friends and the workers. Pettifur closed the factory for the day out of respect and they had a real knees-up in the canteen out at Catberry-on-the-Brink in the evening. I don't normally attend the wakes but Horace's grandkittens' band were playing and I'm a bit of a fan.'

'Is that Gums and Noses?' asked Tilly.

'Yes, that's right. Dandy Nosepeg and Grace Slink are Catberrys on vocals and guitar, then they've got Crusty Catsick and Foxglove Nipton on bass and drums, who also work at the factory. Obviously they're all stage names, but they're building quite a reputation for themselves with their Punk-Goth fusion. There's a rumour that they've been invited to support the Travelling Whoopsies on a national tour.'

The trials and tribulations of an undertaker and Morbid's love of Goth music were swiftly put on hold as Molly Bloom approached with Morbid's fish and chips and Bruiser's omelette. 'There you go,' she said, 'but mind – those plates are hot. Dolly is bringing the livers out in a minute, as she's creaming the mash, so she is.'

Tilly could listen to Molly Bloom's lyrical Irish accent for ever, and was pleased that she had decided to linger and pass the time of day in spite of being so busy. 'So how have you all been these past weeks?' she said. 'I was only saying to Dolly that we'd not seen you. I suppose the weather has kept the crimes down in the town, although if we'd been in Donegal and shut in, I've no doubt that murders would have occurred on the domestic front. No cat likes being cooped up for long. I was beginning to think we'd have to close the café until things picked up, but today we've been as busy as ever thank goodness.'

Dolly arrived with Hettie and Tilly's lunches and Molly melted away back into her kitchen, collecting dirty dishes from the tables on the way. The four cats tucked into their food, saying very little until their plates were clean. There was barely time to come up for air before Dolly arrived with the desserts and every-one noticed that Bruiser had extra chocolate crispies in his rice pudding, clearly a benefit of walking out with the waitress.

After much lip-smacking and purrs of approval, the four cats were ready to face the afternoon. Mor-bid pushed her empty pudding bowl away from her and checked her watch. 'Well, I'd better be making tracks,' she said, getting to her feet and pulling her purse out of her pocket. 'I'll settle up on my way out. I don't want to be late collecting Angus and Columbine Tweed – a nice, neat suicide pact. They even sent full instructions for their funerals with a cheque to cover it. An excellent example of forward thinking.'

'How did they die?' asked Tilly, looking rather shocked.

'I gather they chose to overdose on catnip, then drowned themselves in their bath together. Angus was on his way out anyway and Columbine didn't want to face the future without him. They've even gone for the two in a coffin range.'

On that happy note, Morbid paid up at Dolly's till and left Hettie, Tilly and Bruiser to decide on their next move regarding the Chocolate Corpses Case, as it would soon become known.

Chapter Eight

The drive after lunch out to Catberry-on-the-Brink was far less hazardous than the day before. The water from the overflowing ditches had receded, leaving the roads much clearer, and Bruiser made good time on Miss Scarlet. Hettie had decided to report Morbid Balm's observations on the bodies found in the vat in a face-to-face conversation with Pettifur Catberry before starting an endless round of interviews with the family and workers at the chocolate factory.

On arriving at Catberry Manor, Hettie sent Bruiser off to the factory to take a good look round and to explore the various departments and different methods of production. She was keener to focus on the family dynamics and the possibility of someone being able to identify the female ginger cat or the personal effects that Morbid had found amongst the chocolate corpses. Her head was bursting with questions as Sparks showed her and Tilly into the library, where Pettifur was working on some papers at his desk.

'Please take seats by the fire,' said Pettifur. 'This old house gets so cold at this time of year, even without the rain. If I had my way, I'd live somewhere where the sun shone all year round and there was no need for fires.'

'So do you wish you weren't the head of Catberrys?' asked Hettie, settling herself into an armchair, a bit put out Pettifur wasn't joining them.

He shook his head. 'No, of course not. I'd hoped to have a little longer to enjoy life before I took over the reins from my father but it simply wasn't to be. Anyway, what have you managed to glean so far from your investigations?'

Hettie outlined all Morbid's findings as Pettifur became more and more horrified and Tilly followed up by showing him the personal effects that Morbid had found in the chocolate. Pettifur barely gave them a second glance, distracted by the enormity of what Hettie had just told him. Tilly put the items back in her satchel before finding a clean page in her notebook.

'Four bodies, you say? How can any of this have happened? And more importantly, how long has it been going on?' said Pettifur, putting his head in his paws. 'That vat has been used to make The Tabby in Black range for the past ten years. I can't even begin to think what this all means for the business and the reputation of Catberrys' chocolate. I'm going to have to recall all the stock from the shops and supermarkets. There are thousands and thousands of boxes out there, and then there's the TV ads – I'll have to get those stopped as well.'

Hettie noted that Pettifur was genuinely distressed about the real possibility of the contamination of his chocolate but offered no sympathy for the dead cats involved. She decided to ignore his concerns over the business and pull him back to the reality of identifying the bodies and who might have put them into the vat. 'Morbid Balm suspects that the most recent body of the female ginger cat may have been murdered before being put into the chocolate,' she said. 'Has anyone gone missing in the last few weeks? Perhaps a factory worker or someone in the canteen? Or even a member of your family?'

Pettifur looked puzzled by the question and waved it away with his paw, still distracted by the immensity of the problem he now had to deal with. 'Murder? No, I doubt it. It all sounds like a regrettable accident but if you'll excuse me I have some urgent calls to make. I'll have to put a stop to The Tabby in Black production line. There may be traces of chocolate from the old contaminated vat. I've no idea what to tell the staff. If this gets out we're done for.'

Hettie could see that he was drowning in his own misery, but she was determined to finish her conversation before Pettifur set up his damage limitation campaign. 'Perhaps if there'd been only one body in the vat it might easily have been an accident, but three more suggests that they were put there on purpose.

We may even have a serial killer on our paws.' Hettie put on her authoritative voice. 'I can appreciate what impact all of this has on your business but I think you owe it to your workers and family to allow us to investigate properly. It would be helpful if we could talk to other members of the family and to your workers.'

'But that means everyone will find out about the bodies in the chocolate!' protested Pettifur. 'All I need is one of the workers to go to the *Daily Snout* with this and it will create a national panic.' He reached across his desk and waved a piece of paper under Hettie's nose. 'Look,' he said. 'Here are the sales figures for The Tabby in Black selection from Christmas. They've outsold all our other lines three times over. I just can't allow it to get out that there are feline remains in the chocolate. I'm happy to pay you well if you can come up with a way of protecting the business and all the jobs that would be at risk.'

'But what about the bodies?' demanded Hettie. 'They surely deserve some respect? They are currently in boxes at Shroud and Trestle with no hope of a decent burial unless we find out who they were – and to do that we're going to have to ask the right questions. You might also need to consider that someone may be trying to put you out of business and they could try again if we hush this up.'

Pettifur stood up, pushing his chair away from him looking thunderous; his normal jovial demeanour had entirely deserted him. 'What exactly do you mean?' he hissed.

'I mean that contaminating your chocolates could be the act of an enemy or a rival who wants to close you down,' said Hettie, getting angry, 'and if you have any suspicions as to who that might be, we could bring this case to an end and discover who the bodies belong to. So do you have any enemies capable of a spot of industrial espionage, for want of a better description?'

Pettifur was taken aback by Hettie's change of temperament and so was Tilly. Hettie was often grumpy, and even more often sarcastic, but she was rarely angry, particularly with a client.

'I'm sorry,' said Pettifur, slumping down on the chair behind his desk. 'I just can't see a way out of this nightmare. Forgive me, but I honestly can't think of anyone vindictive enough to put the whole business at risk.'

'Perhaps you could call a staff and family meeting to let everyone know what has happened, then ask them to keep it to themselves until we complete our investigations?' suggested Tilly, who had been quietly scribbling in her notepad. 'You could explain that if word got out their jobs would be in danger. Being honest with them might make them more helpful in sorting everything out.'

Pettifur and Hettie both looked at Tilly as if the sun had suddenly emerged from the rain clouds. Her words of wisdom reminded Hettie that Tilly might seem detached during her interviews but her friend was a peacemaker whose thought process was as sharp as a razor and fuelled by common sense.

'That's an excellent idea,' said Pettifur. 'I'll call a meeting in the canteen for all staff this afternoon and I'll tell the family members not working at the factory this evening. As it's Friday, we all sit down to dinner together and that will be the best time to broach the subject. Perhaps you might like to join us and I can introduce you to them?'

Hettie was rather hoping for a takeaway supper from Elsie Haddock's fish shop, in front of a fire with an episode of *The Beverly Hillbillies* on TV, but she could see the sense in meeting the rest of the Catberry family before interviewing them as potential murderers. 'That would be lovely,' she said. 'What time would you like us?'

'Splendid,' said Pettifur, looking a little more cheerful. 'Shall we say seven for seven-thirty? We always enjoy a drink in the orangery before dinner, a custom my father used to insist upon, and I think my mother appreciates us keeping up the family traditions. Now, if you'll excuse me, I must go and find Oliver and get him to organise the staff meeting. I'll send a car for you both for six forty-five if you give me your address.'

It was a rare thing for Hettie and Tilly to be asked for their address and even rarer that a client would send a car for them. The Butters' Bakery didn't sound quite right as an address for a detective agency, but it was Hettie's quick-thinking this time that dug them out of a hole. 'We have another meeting at an address in the town's high street later so shall we say outside the post office?'

'Perfect,' said Pettifur, crossing to the door. 'I'll see you out.'

Pettifur marched Hettie and Tilly to the front door. Grabbing an umbrella from the hatstand, he let them out into the drive and set off towards the factory. Miss Scarlet was parked where Bruiser had left her and the two cats headed for the sidecar, keen to get out of the rain. It was only a matter of minutes before Bruiser arrived, fresh from Oliver Crumbwell's guided tour of the chocolate factory.

Chapter Nine

By the time that Hettie, Tilly and Bruiser arrived back at the bakery, the Butter sisters had wiped down their surfaces and shut up for the day, having sold out of almost everything. Hettie was keen to hear what Bruiser had to say about his visit to the factory and Tilly was nervously biting her claws, wondering if they had enough clean, respectable clothes to wear for the Catberry dinner.

They made their way round to the back door, letting themselves in on a party atmosphere by the bread ovens. Betty and Beryl had their radio turned up to full volume as they danced and sang to the *Hits of the Sixties* programme. The fact that they were back in business had lightened their spirits and they were both busy rolling out pastry and cooking pie fillings in their preparation area.

It was Betty who noticed them first and rushed to turn the radio down, muting the 1910 Fruitgum Company's rendition of 'Yummy, Yummy, Yummy'. Beryl offered another chorus before realising that she was on her own with it. 'I've put a box of cakes in your room,' Betty said, wiping her paws on her apron. 'We only had a few left so we decided to shut up shop and crack on with the baking for tomorrow. We've had a bit of a stampede today but it was good to see folks out and about again.'

'Yes, the high street was much busier and Bloomers was packed,' said Tilly, passing Betty's golfing umbrella back to her. 'We've been invited to Catberry Manor for dinner with the family tonight and I'm not sure we've got anything to wear.'

'Well, we could stump up a couple of gold lamé cocktail dresses if they're any use? Figure-hugging and stretchy,' said Beryl. 'I was going to take them down to Jessie's charity shop but you're welcome to them.'

'That's very kind,' said Tilly, 'but I don't think it's the weather for gold lamé. I'm sure I can find something.'

Tilly also doubted that her friend Jessie would have too many takers for gold lamé; she regularly sat in at her shop when Jessie was away buying stock and had a very good idea about what sold and what didn't.

'And are you invited as well?' asked Betty, looking at Bruiser. 'You'll have to get your best waistcoat out if you're sitting down with the Catberrys.'

Bruiser shook his head. 'No, me an' Dolly is off ta the pictures ta see *The Wicker Cat*. Dolly likes anythin' pagan or Celtic, wot with 'er bein' Cornish.'

'Pettifur Catberry is sending a car for us,' said Hettie, 'which means Bruiser has the night off.'

'Sending a car!' mimicked Beryl. 'Sounds like you've got your slingbacks under the Catberry table there. Oh my, we shall have to make an appointment to talk to you next, you're such high flyers.'

Tilly giggled, mainly at the thought of Hettie wearing slingbacks, and opened the door to their room, leaving the Butters to their baking. Hettie put the kettle on and Bruiser helpfully lit the fire while Tilly plundered the bottom drawer of their filing cabinet, where she kept all their clothes. Cardigans, shirts, a multitude of odd socks and several pairs of trousers were dragged out onto the floor for general inspection, as well as Hettie's best jacket – or, more especially, her only one.

'Some of this stuff needs sponging,' said Tilly. 'I've still got gravy down the front of my best cardigan from Christmas, and look – there's a sugared almond in the pocket.' She picked the fluff off the sweet and put it in her mouth, sucking on it loudly as she carried on sorting the clothes.

Hettie prepared three mugs of milky tea before investigating the box of cakes that the Butters had left for them. 'Looks like there's two each,' she said. 'Two custard slices, a cream horn, an egg custard and two ring donuts.'

'I don't care what I have as long as I have the cream horn,' said Tilly, doing her best to sponge the gravy off her best cardigan in their small sink.

'I'm 'appy with anythin',' said Bruiser, sitting down on the rug in front of the fire.

'Right then,' said Hettie, 'I'll have a custard slice and a donut. Tilly can have the egg custard to go with the cream horn, and Bruiser, you can have the same as me. How does that sound?'

There were claws up all round and the three cats settled to their afternoon tea, enjoying every mouthful of the box of cakes. When tea was over, Bruiser gave his impressions of the chocolate factory and Hettie and Tilly listened intently. 'It's quite some operation they got there,' he began. 'That Oliver cat showed me round. 'E said they'd just invested in a load of new equipment an' gone completely electric. The old vats of chocolate, like the one they found the bodies in, were heated by gas flames underneath them, but now they just switch the new ones on and the chocolate reaches the correct temperature before they start pourin' it into moulds over the different flavours. Then the chocolates all come down a giant conveyor belt, where workers pick 'em out ta fill up the boxes. They do a different batch of chocolates each day so they don't get the products mixed up. Today was Creamy Egg day, so I watched as they all got packed up in boxes, then shrink-wrapped and stacked on pallets.'

'Shrink-wrapped?' interrupted Tilly. 'Why would they shrink Creamy Eggs?'

Bruiser laughed. 'They don't shrink the eggs. They box 'em up and put 'em in this giant machine that stretches cling film across 'em an' seals 'em ready for deliverin' ta the shops. Magic, really.'

'So they do a different sort of chocolate every day?' clarified Hettie. 'How do they decide what to do next?'

'Oliver said it depends on the orders but tomorrow is Tabby in Black day, as they do that every Saturday just ta keep up with the demand – it's their most successful product. 'E said they're workin' Sundays up till Easter, as Sundays is when they do Easter eggs.'

'How exciting,' said Tilly, who often helped with the town's Easter Egg hunt. In previous years, she'd been so carried away with hiding them that by the time the town's kittens went out in search of them, she had quite forgotten where she'd put them. Only recently, one of Tilly's eggs had turned up behind the cricket pavilion on the recreation ground and had been there for at least two years judging by the sell-by date.

'What was the security like?' asked Hettie. 'I'm wondering how easy it would be for an outsider to access the production areas, especially the vats?'

'Well, Oliver spotted me straight away. I didn't get any further than the despatch area before 'e was on me ta ask what I was doin' there. Them new vats 'as lids, too – 'e pointed that out ta me.'

'So how difficult would it be to dump a body in one of those old vats, now you've seen the factory set-up?'

'I'd say it would 'ave ta be an inside job for a strong cat, unless the victim was still alive and climbed up the ladder before they was shoved in. They'd 'ave ta do it when the factory was shut down as there's loads of cats about in workin' hours. Oliver said they start at seven in the mornin' an' finish at six, when everythin' is shut down, but they're workin' seven days a week at the moment. 'E said they got an alarm system an' a night watch cat ta keep the place secure.'

'Maybe the bodies were put in the vat after it had been moved to the despatch area?' suggested Tilly. 'If they were murdered, perhaps the killer had stored them up waiting for an opportunity to get rid of them and when they heard that the vats were going for scrap they stuck them in there. I expect there's vans coming in and out of that packing area all day long. One of them could have transported the bodies to the vat while no one was looking.'

'That's a very good point,' said Hettie, 'but I can't help but think that there are easier ways of getting rid of bodies, and except for the ginger cat the other bodies are quite old. Why would you want to store a body until it became a skeleton? Of course, if you're right, then Pettifur has nothing to worry about as his chocolates won't have been contaminated – but I don't think this case is going to bring him a happy ending somehow.'

Bruiser checked his pocket watch and stood up. 'If yer don't need me any more, I'll get goin'. I'll 'ave ta spruce meself up fer Dolly – she's cookin' me a bit of tea at Bloomers before we go ta the cinema. Will we be goin' back ta Catberrys tomorrow?'

'I expect so,' said Hettie. 'That's if we survive dinner this evening. I'll come and find you in the morning when we know what we're doing.'

'Right'o.'

Bruiser left Hettie and Tilly sorting through their clothes. Tilly eventually decided on her sponged-down best royal blue cardigan and her business slacks, which seemed to have shrunk around the waistband since Christmas. After much muttering, Hettie chose a plain, slightly creased white shirt with her best jacket to go over it and her own pair of business slacks.

'I think we need to go and buy some new things from Jessie's charity shop,' said Tilly. 'She's got a new Tabby Chic range that I wouldn't mind having a look at. We don't have enough posh clothes – or maybe we could go to Malkin and Sprinkle's sale?'

'Maybe,' said Hettie, a little distracted by the pile of newspapers stacked against the staff sideboard where Tilly kept anything she thought might be useful. 'How far back do these go?'

'Why? What are you looking for?'

'I just wondered if we still had the paper reporting Horace Catberry's funeral? All the family turned out for it and we're about to meet them all, so I thought we could familiarise ourselves with them.'

Tilly joined Hettie on the floor to sort through the pile of *Daily Snouts*, eventually striking gold. 'Here it is!' she said triumphantly. 'All over the front page, with more inside.'

The image on the front page reminded Hettie of an old Victorian school photograph: the Catberry family all lined up in their best black funeral clothes, like some macabre football team. Pettifur and Morgana were in the centre, flanked by some of the older female members of the family. The next generation looked a little less sombre but equally bizarre for such a posed record of Horace's big day. It was as if they were ghosts, ready to walk out of the picture at any moment.

'Blimey!' said Hettie. 'The Munsters ride again! You wouldn't want to meet any of them on a dark night, and look at the headline: "Farewell to the Real Tabby in Black!". I suppose that older cat next to Pettifur is Praline, the widow, and those other two standing beside her must be Lolly and Rhubarb, her daughters. I see that Oliver Crumbwell has been relegated to the back row and I assume those two younger cats are the Goth sisters, Grace and Dandy. Not exactly a family photo to treasure but at least they got a free front page ad out of it. I bet there was a rush to buy The Tabby in Black selection. I wonder if they created a special funeral edition at the factory out of respect for Horace's demise?'

Tilly giggled at Hettie's irreverence and turned to the inside pages where there was a full report of the funeral with more photographs, including one of Pettifur Catberry helping his distressed mother out of the grave. 'Prunella Snap did well to capture that image,' said Hettie, 'and it's more in focus than her usual contributions to the *Daily Snout*. I wonder if she'll be including that one in the paper's desk calendar for next year?'

'There's a bit here about how Horace died,' said Tilly. 'It says that he was taking tea in his library when the telephone rang on his desk, which made him jump and choke on the Mog Nob he'd just dipped in his cup. Praline Catberry was dozing by the fire and didn't realise he was choking. By the time she'd woken up it was too late.'

'What a load of nonsense!' said Hettie. 'For a start, why didn't she wake up when the telephone rang? And if he'd just dunked his Mog Nob in his tea, it surely must have been soft enough for him to swallow without difficulty. I'm beginning to find Horace Catberry's death a bit confusing – and then there was the palaver over not viewing the body that Morbid told us about and all the stuff that Praline put in the coffin. That's pretty strange behaviour for a grieving widow.'

'They do say that grief affects cats in many different ways,' Tilly pointed out. 'Maybe she just wanted to keep him to herself after he'd died? It must have been a shock and choking is a horrible way to go. She must have felt guilty that she couldn't save him.'

'Well, maybe she didn't want to save him,' said Hettie. 'I can't wait to meet her. Come on – let's get our glad rags on. We'd better get ourselves across the road to the post office – it's nearly a quarter to seven.'

Chapter Ten

The Rolls-Royce was waiting outside the post office as Hettie and Tilly emerged into the high street. Considering the state and tangle of clothes that Tilly had rescued from the filing cabinet, the two cats had scrubbed up well: Hettie hid the creases in her shirt with her jacket and Tilly looked almost smart in her sponged-down cardigan. On seeing them crossing the road from the bakery, the chauffeur leapt out of the car and opened the back door to allow them to slide into the comfort of the back seat. 'Perks at your service,' he said, doffing his cap as he closed the door and retook his place in the driver's seat.

Perks looked suspiciously like Sparks, Pettifur's butler and during the course of the journey Hettie established that they were in fact brothers. 'How long have you worked for the Catberrys?' she asked, finding the silence a little awkward as she and Tilly languished in the comfort of the heated leather seats.

'Born to it, I suppose you could say,' said the cat, keeping his eyes on the road ahead. 'My father was chauffeur to Mr Sylvester Catberry and Mr Horace until he got too old to drive. Finished his days at Sunny Tails, the factory's retirement home. I took over from him at the same time as my brother Sparks got to be butler up at the Manor. He replaced my Uncle Ned, who retired at the same time as my father. My mother was housekeeper to the Catberrys and our grandfather worked for Hauxston Catberry – all long gone now, sadly, but you could say we've been in chocolate for generations.'

The comment was unfortunate, bearing in mind what had so recently been found 'in' the chocolate, but Perks was keen to talk and Hettie seized the opportunity to find out a little more about the family. 'How did you find Horace Catberry? Was he a good boss?'

'One of the best,' said Perks, without any hesitation. 'He was driven, if you know what I mean, and no pun intended. He loved his life and his business, took a proper pride in his achievements, and really looked after anyone who worked for him, just like his father before him. We were all devastated when he died. He was the sort of cat you expected to live for ever.'

'And what about Praline Catberry? It must have been a terrible shock for her,' suggested Hettie, gently probing the subject of Horace's death.

'She bore it like the lady she is,' said Perks. 'They were a team and after Mr Horace died she reluctantly stepped back to give Mr Pettifur a clear run at it. She's rarely seen these days, which is sad as she was so full of life and interested in everything. She's still queen of the family, though, which has put a few noses out of joint.'

Hettie was about to ask Perks what he meant but the Rolls Royce had swung into the driveway of Catberry Manor and the conversation was abruptly brought to a conclusion as Perks parked and sprang out of his seat to open the door for them. The rain had started again and Sparks met them with a large umbrella, seeing them safely into the Manor as his brother drove off to the garages, where he had a rather nice flat.

Sparks wasted no time in showing the newly arrived guests into the orangery, which lived up to its name. The glass conservatory was bursting with tall exotic plants, some with fruit and others with giant leaves that touched the roof. Tilly gasped at the size of everything. The plants dwarfed the gathering of cats, who had congregated in the centre of the room by a table laden with bottles of sherry and plates of dainty sweet and savoury pastries. The view from the windows, although slightly obscured by vegetation, was breathtaking, even in the rain. An avenue of elm trees reached into the distance, culminating in a Gothic folly which drew the eye immediately. The trees were flanked by formal gardens, alive with snowdrops, Christmas roses and the promise of daffodils – still in bud and keeping their flowers to themselves until the rain finally stopped.

Pettifur broke away from the group to welcome Hettie and Tilly. He looked very smart in his black tie dinner suit and Oliver Crumbwell was equally well turned out. The rest of the assembled family was all female; centre stage, a tall, strikingly elegant older cat – every bit the mistress of the manor – was leaning on an ornate, silver-topped, ebony walking stick. The stick was the only indication of her age and she made Morgana look like a tawdry stage actress, desperately trying to hold her position as Pettifur's wife and Praline Catberry's successor as first lady of chocolate.

Tilly decided to have a shy moment and hide behind Hettie as Pettifur did the introductions, announcing them as Miss Bagshot and Miss Jenkins from the world-famous No. 2 Feline Detective Agency. The older cats nodded, looking curiously at the two strangers, then carried on talking amongst themselves, but the two youngest cats in the room – wearing identical short black tunics with Dr. Martens boots – rushed over to offer their paws. Grace and Dandy possessed none of the aloof restraint that radiated from the rest of the family and were keen to welcome the new arrivals.

'Hi!' said Dandy. 'It's so cool to meet some real detectives. I've seen some of the stuff you've done in the papers. Pops says you're working on a case for us at the moment? We're dying to know what it is.'

'Weren't you at the staff meeting this afternoon?' Hettie asked, assuming that the gathering had gone ahead.

'No,' said Grace, keen to enter the conversation. 'We gave it a miss – we were gigging last night and

Pops gave us the day off so we went into the town to buy some stage gear. We got some amazing threads at that charity shop in Cheapcuts Lane.'

'That's run by my friend Jessie,' said Tilly, feeling more at ease with the younger cats. 'I sometimes sit in for her when she's away buying stock.'

'She's got a great shop there,' said Dandy. 'A whole rail of black stuff and some really neat lace-up Gothic corsets, perfect for the stage. I wouldn't mind working there myself if I wasn't up to my neck in seasonal chocolate lines.'

'I gather your band is doing well,' said Hettie. 'I've been hearing good things about it. Are you planning to go professional?'

Grace shook her head. 'Pops would have a heart attack if we did that. Me and Dandy are next in line to inherit unless Morgana springs a surprise on us and has a bunch of kittens.'

'And how do you feel about that?' asked Hettie. 'Running a business like Catberrys must be a huge responsibility.'

The maid who'd served Hettie and Tilly afternoon tea cut short the conversation by offering them a glass of sherry. Tilly waved it away, as she'd never got on with it and thought the taste was nasty, but Hettie indulged herself, mainly to keep up appearances in sophisticated company. She gulped the sherry down in one, hoping that a refill wouldn't be offered.

Pettifur put paid to that prospect by clapping his paws together to get everyone's attention. 'I suppose you're all wondering why we have detectives at dinner tonight?' he said. A murmur went round the family and Pettifur continued, 'The fact is Oliver made a terrible discovery on Wednesday. He found what has turned out to be four bodies in the outgoing Tabby in Black vat.'

There was an audible gasp from the family and Hettie and Tilly watched closely for their reactions. The Goth cats looked positively delighted at the macabre find but Praline, Lolly and Rhubarb clung to each other in horror. It was clear to Hettie that Oliver hadn't shared his discovery with his wife and that she hadn't attended the staff meeting; in fact, Rhubarb seemed more disturbed than any of them. Morgana looked smug, as if her prior knowledge of the bodies put her above the rest of her in-laws.

'Miss Bagshot and Miss Jenkins,' Pettifur continued, 'have so far established that three of the bodies are skeletons and appear to have been in the vat for some time – but the fourth body was, for want of a better word, intact and possibly identifiable. The body is of a female ginger cat and it appears that she might have been murdered.'

'Enough!' shouted Praline, thumping her stick down on the floor to get everyone's attention. 'Pettifur, that is quite sufficient. How dare you make this announcement without coming to me first? And in front of strangers too.' She jabbed her stick in Hettie and Tilly's direction. 'Regardless of your new-found status, I am still head of this family and will be until the day I die. You are only where you are because of the hard work and sacrifices made by your father and his fathers before him. Be in no doubt – I am here to protect that legacy and you will answer to me on anything and everything that concerns this business. Is that understood? And that goes for the rest of you. From now on, you all owe your living and lifestyle to me.'

Hettie and Tilly were quite taken aback by Praline's very public rebuke of her only son. The speech seemed to have been brewing for some time; it was certainly enough to wipe the smugness from Morgana's face, as well as shocking the rest of the family. Pettifur hung his head like a scolded young kitten; his humiliation had taken away all the authority that he'd fought to gain since his father's unexpected death. Morgana stepped forward and took his arm, summoning up some wifely support, but no one else moved and Praline's words hung uncomfortably over them all.

Sparks broke the silence by announcing that dinner was served but only Praline responded. 'I will take dinner in my rooms, Sparks, and leave this apology for a family to dine on their own inadequacies.'

'Very good,' the butler said, as Praline made her way to the door. Lolly followed like the attentive daughter she was, only to be dismissed by a rather aggressive wave of her mother's walking stick, and the family was left to stare as Praline slammed the door shut behind her, turning her exit into a brilliant piece of theatre. It was Dandy who broke the silence. 'Isn't Granny magnificent?' she said. 'What a legend!'

'Yeah,' said Grace, 'no prisoners taken there but what about these bodies? How exciting is that?'

Pettifur ignored his daughters' comments and led the way into the dining room, which was next to the orangery. Hettie and Tilly followed at the rear of the deflated family; only Grace and Dandy looked like they were really enjoying themselves.

Their father took his place at the head of the long table, with Morgana to his right. Sparks offered the chairs on Pettifur's left to Hettie and Tilly and Lolly sat down next to them. Tilly had hoped to be sitting next to Dandy and Grace but they ended up opposite her with Oliver and Rhubarb. Sparks hastily cleared away the cutlery and glasses from the other end of the table, where Praline normally sat.

There was very little conversation during the soup course. Everyone seemed to be concentrating on spooning it into their mouths, as if a vow of silence had come into force. Tilly took extra care to make sure she didn't splash her newly sponged cardigan and Hettie waited patiently for Pettifur to pick up the subject of the bodies that had been so brutally terminated by his mother.

When the empty bowls had been cleared away, Morgana reinstated the conversation in the most inappropriate manner. 'Well, what a bunch of scaredy-cats you all are,' she said. 'The mighty bloody Catberrys being squashed underfoot by an ageing matriarch who refuses to retire to her own old cats' home. How sweet it would be if she just packed her expensive luggage and moved into Sunny Tails, where she could dribble her venom all day long while the rest of you get on with the business of running – or ruining – the family firm.'

'My dear,' said Pettifur, putting his paw on hers to stem the vitriolic flow. 'We're all upset but your being rude about my mother doesn't help.'

'I call that outburst more than rude,' said Lolly, getting to her feet. 'You bust your way into my brother's life and affections, taking him away from the business on an extended honeymoon. You happily accept all the good things that our family fortune has brought you. You sit around all day, preening yourself or splashing Pettifur's money around in the most expensive shops you can find – and then you sit at our table, eating our food and insulting our mother, who accepted you into this family because – and only because – you were Pettifur's choice.'

Morgana wrenched her paw away from Pettifur's, then stood up and walked behind his chair, past Hettie and Tilly, to land a slap across Lolly's face. Lolly responded by slapping her back, narrowly missing Tilly, who managed to duck out of the way. Pettifur stood up and shouted for them both to sit down but his words fell on deaf ears as the two cats engaged in a ferocious fight. The white cloth became speckled with blood as they rolled, hissed and spat their way down the table, knocking plates, cutlery, bread rolls, bowls of flowers and glasses to the floor.

Hettie and Tilly got up from their places and stood back to watch the spectacle, as Dandy and Grace cheered the fighters on. At Rhubarb's suggestion, Oliver tried to separate them but was sent spinning across the room, colliding with a grand piano by the French windows.

Sparks brought matters to a conclusion by entering the dining room carrying a large joint of roast beef, accompanied by all the trimmings. Morgana hit the platter head-on, sending her crashing into the skirting board and momentarily knocking her out. She lay surrounded by roast potatoes, parsnips and Yorkshire puddings, the beef finding sanctuary on top of her head as the juices trickled down into her ears.

Lolly limped from the room, licking her wounds, quickly followed by Oliver and Rhubarb. Dandy and Grace applied themselves to salvaging some of the dinner from the floor and Pettifur attended to Morgana, who was now sitting up and sobbing – more for her ruined designer dress than the loss of the fight she'd engaged in with Lolly.

When the dust, blood and gravy had settled, Hettie thought she might comment on the situation. It was clear to her that the dinner party was over. 'I wonder if we might ask for a car to take us back into the town?' she asked, above the sobbing noise that Morgana was making. 'We can see that things have become a little difficult this evening so maybe you should call us tomorrow if you still require our services?'

'Yes, of course,' said Pettifur, leaving Morgana in a heap on the floor. 'Please forgive my family. I fear the news about the bodies may have detonated an unexploded bomb of concerns amongst them. A delayed reaction to my father's death, perhaps.'

'Come off it, Pops,' said Dandy, who had managed to fill a plate with the scattered roast vegetables and was sitting down at the table to eat them. 'No point trying to make out that it's Grandpa's death that's caused all this. You know that Granny hates Morgana. She always has. It was Grandpa who welcomed her because he fancied her himself, and Lolly and Rhubarb don't like her either. You all need to get real.'

'Yeah, and I want to know more about these bodies,' added Grace, as she too filled a plate and pulled a chair up next to her sister. 'This family is a train crash anyway but bodies in the chocolate make things much more interesting.'

Sparks, who'd been standing by Morgana after carefully removing the joint of beef from her head, decided to help his master out of the situation. 'Would you like me to call Perks and have him bring the car round for our visitors, sir?' he said.

Pettifur was instantly grateful, fearing what his daughters may come out with next, and nodded his consent. Sparks indicated to Hettie and Tilly to follow him out of the room, leaving the carnage behind them. He picked up the phone in the hall and dialled his brother's number.

By the time Sparks had escorted them to the front door, Perks was waiting in the Rolls-Royce. Hettie and Tilly clambered into the back seat and were quickly whisked away and back into the town. This time they travelled in silence; all three cats knew that the evening hadn't been a success. As they entered the high street, Hettie asked Perks to pull over. 'Just here will do nicely,' she said, wanting to make a swift exit and tugging at Tilly's cardigan. 'Thank you for bringing us home.' The two friends made their way out of the car before Perks had time to open the door for them. He doffed his cap and drove away, leaving Hettie and Tilly to scamper across the road and into Elsie Haddock's fish and chip shop, minutes before Elsie was due to switch her fryers off for the evening.

'You're lucky,' she said. 'I was about to put my feet up in front of the telly. I've got two cod and a couple of portions of chips left – and a bag of batter bits if you're interested? I'm keeping the hake for mine and Squeak's supper, as she's been out all day delivering post. She's been worked off her feet with Lavender Stamp being away.'

'Cod and chips with batter bits would be lovely,' said Tilly. 'Is Squeak enjoying being Lavender's postcat?'

'I wouldn't say enjoying,' said Elsie, as she parcelled up the fish and chips, 'but my niece is a hard worker and she doesn't have time for Lavender's tantrums. She enjoys being out and about, seeing folk on her rounds, although this weather has been awful for her. She comes home dripping wet sometimes, but she never complains.'

Hettie tucked the parcel of fish and chips under her arm and Tilly settled up with the fifty pence piece she kept in her cardigan pocket for emergencies, slightly sticky from the sugared almond that had been keeping it company. Elsie passed over the change and saw them out, turning the closed sign round on the door. The two cats scampered home with their supper, avoiding as many puddles as possible. There was much to talk about in front of their fire.

Chapter Eleven

'Words fail me,' said Hettie, poking the final chip into her mouth as Tilly added another shovel of coal to the fire. 'Grace was spot on when she said her family was a train crash. I couldn't have put it better myself.'

The two cats had enjoyed their supper and the tail end of *The Beverly Hillbillies* on TV, without any discussion featuring the Catberrys, but now it was time to settle down and review the last couple of days. 'I'm not sure if we'll be invited back to investigate those deaths,' said Tilly, pulling her notepad out of her satchel. 'It seems to me that chocolate-covered corpses are the least of that family's worries.'

'I agree. They'll probably end up killing each other if this evening was anything to go by and Praline Catberry is quite something – you really wouldn't want to cross her.'

'I feel sorry for Pettifur,' said Tilly. 'He's just trying to do his best but calling us in before he'd told his mother about the bodies probably wasn't his best idea. And she's got a point too.'

'In what way?'

'Well, if you'd been running things for as long as she has, it's only right that she should be kept informed if anything goes wrong. Perks the chauffeur said that Praline and Horace were a team so the business must still mean a lot to her.'

'Certainly more than it means to Morgana, that's for sure,' said Hettie, reaching for her catnip pipe. 'I don't know what possessed Pettifur to hook up with her. She obviously hates the business and everyone associated with it. If we were drawing up a suspects list, she'd be right at the top of it as far as the most recent body is concerned.'

'But that doesn't explain the skeletons,' Tilly pointed out. 'Morbid seemed to think they'd been dead for some time and Morgana is quite new to the family.'

'Let's draw up a list of cats we'd like to interview,' said Hettie, blowing the perfect smoke ring into the fire. 'I don't think we should spend too much time on it at the moment as Pettifur may decide to pull the rug from under us. It's only Dandy and Grace who seem interested in the bodies anyway. The rest of them are too busy being at war with each other.'

'And Pettifur,' Tilly added.

'Yes, but even he might be double bluffing. I get the feeling that he's not entirely pleased with inheriting and carrying on his father's legacy, especially after the impact it's had on his relationship with Morgana.'

Tilly flicked through her notes before finding a clean page to write down a list of potential interviewees. 'I'll put Pettifur at the top, and then Morgana, as they both might be suspects; then Lolly and Rhubarb and Oliver Crumbwell, as he seems to know everything about the family and the factory and as he's the manager he'd have access at all times to the vats. I'm going to put Johnny Clash down, as he works in the despatch area, and Crusty Catsick, as she's in packing – and the Goth band, of course.'

'What about the other band member? What was her name?'

Tilly looked through her notes until she came to Morbid's page. 'Ah, here it is – Foxglove Nipton. Morbid said she works at the factory but I'm not sure what she does. I'll add Grace and Dandy too – they seem very happy to talk to us.'

'Yes, and they're wonderfully indiscreet,' Hettie pointed out. 'We'll probably get more out of them than the rest of the family put together. Put Sparks and Perks down as well. They've obviously been with the family a long time and servants are usually reliable for spilling the beans.'

'That just leaves Praline from the cats we know about,' said Tilly, 'although I doubt that she'll talk to us. She seemed furious that we were there at all tonight.'

'I know what you mean but out of all the cats on your list she's the most interesting,' said Hettie. 'There's all that stuff Morbid told us about filling up Horace's coffin and not letting the family pay their respects and then her leaping into the grave at his funeral – not to mention that ridiculous article in the *Daily Snout* about how he died. I don't know how we could pull it off but if we carry on with the case it's vital that we talk to her.'

'What are we going to do about the identification of the ginger cat's body?' asked Tilly. 'I'm not sure Morbid would want the Catberrys turning up at Shroud and Trestle for a viewing but one of them might recognise her.'

'Good point,' said Hettie. 'We'll have to ask Morbid to photograph her. Not exactly a picture for a family album but it may jog someone's memory along with the personal effects she gave us. I'll call her in the morning.'

'How about a couple of custard creams and a milky tea before we go to sleep?' suggested Tilly, putting her notepad back in her satchel.

'An excellent idea,' said Hettie, knocking her pipe out on the fender.

Back at Catberry Manor, Morgana stared out into the darkness, her tears falling like the raindrops that trickled down the windowpane. There was no escape as the night closed in around her. She nervously pulled at the threads on her dressing gown, knowing that her life couldn't be so easily unpicked.

Chapter Twelve

Hettie and Tilly loved Saturdays, especially if they weren't working on a case. It was a day for staying in their beds until late, enjoying a bacon bap and a frothy coffee from the bakery before sauntering down the high street to Bloomers, where they would take their time over one of Molly Bloom's mixed grills before visiting Jessie in her charity shop. Jessie could be relied upon for the latest gossip and Tilly was always keen to check out any new arrivals in the cardigan department.

'No call from Pettifur then,' said Hettie, draining her frothy coffee mug, which left her with a temporary creamy moustache. 'It looks like we might be off the hook, although I think I'll send him a bill for two days' work. It's not as if he can't afford it.'

'It's a shame not to get to the bottom of the bodies, though,' said Tilly, licking her paws after her bacon bap. 'It could be four murders we're turning our backs on and that doesn't seem right.'

'It could even be five if someone bumped Horace off,' Hettie pointed out. 'The thing about cats with money is that it gives them power to do what they like and usually get away with it.'

'Why do you think Horace might have been murdered?'

'I don't know but it's been bothering me ever since Morbid told us about her services not being required in preparing his body for burial. It's like they just stuck him in his coffin and got him in the ground as quickly as possible. The only reason I can think of is that there was something to hide. Then there's the letters and documents that Praline put in the coffin. I wonder what they were?'

'Well, we'll never know,' said Tilly, 'but it's a neat way of getting rid of stuff.'

'Come on,' said Hettie. 'Let's get on with our Saturday. If our services aren't required by the Catberrys, I know where there are two mixed grills with our names on them – and maybe a look round Jessie's Tabby Chic range afterwards?'

'Ooh lovely!' said Tilly, pulling on her slightly stained Saturday cardigan. 'I'll stick the answerphone on in case Pettifur calls us.'

She clambered into the staff sideboard and emerged seconds later. The two cats put on their macs and stepped out into the high street. 'Looks like Lavender Stamp has returned from her customer awareness course, judging by the queue,' observed Hettie.

The postmistress was renowned for her cantankerous behaviour towards her customers and liked nothing better than to keep cats waiting at her counter. Her pedantic application of post office regulations did little to win over the townsfolk and a visit to her post office was to be endured rather than welcomed. 'I don't know how Squeak puts up with her,' said Tilly. 'It must be the worst job in the world to be Lavender Stamp's postcat.'

'Especially as Lavender's last postcat was murdered,' added Hettie, remembering one of their previous cases. 'Oh look – speak of the devil.'

Squeak emerged from the post office and signalled to them as she crossed the road. 'Glad I caught you,' she said. 'I've got a telegram for you. It's just come in.'

Hettie took the envelope and slit it open with her claw. 'Well, well, well,' she said, casting her eye across it, 'short but sweet. "PLEASE ATTEND ME AT 10AM ON MONDAY NEXT AT CATBERRY MANOR. PRALINE CATBERRY."'

'Straight out of one of them Agatha Crispy books,' said Squeak. 'Catberry Manor sounds a bit frightening. Are they the ones that make the chocolate? I've still got a Tabby in Black selection left over from Christmas that I haven't got round to yet.'

'If I were you I wouldn't bother,' said Hettie. 'It's probably out of date by now.'

Squeak looked puzzled, but as she had a full bag of letters to deliver she went on her way, leaving Hettie and Tilly to ponder over the telegram as they headed for Bloomers.

'I wonder what she wants us for?' said Hettie.

'Maybe she's decided to handle the bodies in the chocolate herself. She made it clear to Pettifur that she was in charge last night and that's probably why he hasn't phoned us.'

'Well, it looks like we'll get our interview with her after all,' said Hettie, pushing the café door open.

Bloomers was busy. Hettie and Tilly headed for their table and slid into their seats. 'Oh look,' said Tilly, 'there's Grace and Dandy on that table over there. I think they've seen us.'

'And they're coming over,' said Hettie. 'So much for a peaceful lunch.'

'Hi,' said Dandy, 'we thought we'd come over to apologise for last night. You can choose your friends, as they say, but you're stuck with your family.'

'Please don't worry,' said Hettie. 'In our job, we've seen far worse. Shouldn't you both be at the factory?'

'No,' said Grace. 'After finding out about the bodies, Granny has shut down the factory until further notice. Pops is furious but she calls the shots.'

Grace and Dandy lingered, giving Tilly no choice but to invite them to share their table just as Dolly Scollop arrived to take their order. 'I don't believe it!' she said, eyeing up Dandy and Grace. 'You're from Gums an' Noses, if I'm not mistaken. I've been to some of your gigs. 'Ansome, they were, an' that drummer knows 'ow to twirl 'er sticks. Are you playin' anywhere local again soon?'

'As a matter of fact, we're gigging at the Cat and Fiddle tonight,' said Dandy, keen to meet a fan. 'You should come along. We could leave your name on the door. Perhaps you'd all like to come?'

'That would be lovely,' said Tilly excitedly, before Hettie had the chance to turn the invitation down. Having run her own band for many years, Hettie was very selective about live music gigs and found it strange to be in the audience rather than on the stage. These days the music had to be really good to convince her to leave her fireside for an evening.

'Great,' said Grace, 'so that's three on the door?'

'Could you stretch to four?' asked Dolly, 'on account of me wantin' to bring my young man?'

Hettie smiled to herself. She'd never heard Bruiser referred to as a young man: he was definitely a cat enjoying his later years, having spent his youth as a wanderer long before meeting Dolly.

'Four's fine,' said Grace. 'The more, the merrier. We've got the manager of the Travelling Whoopsies coming to see us tonight, as we're being considered for the support on their next tour. So don't forget to shout and clap loud after each number.'

'Consider it done,' said Dolly. 'Now, what can I get you?'

'We'll have our usual,' said Tilly, 'and what's for pudding?'

'We've got jam roly-poly with custard or ice cream; Tart Citron – thas' lemon to you an' me – or chocolate traybake with sauce Anglaise, better known as custard. Molly says we ought to go a bit upmarket since she got Delia Sniff's recipe book for Christmas. Mind you, it's just as well that I'm good at translation.'

'I'll have the traybake with custard,' said Hettie.

'The jam roly-poly for me, with ice cream and custard,' added Tilly.

Grace and Dandy were having a good look at the menu and eventually both went for the fish and chips. 'An' what can I get you for pudding, my lovelies?'

'Definitely not the chocolate traybake,' said Dandy. 'I'll go for the lemon tart.'

'Me too,' said Grace.

'Right you are,' said Dolly. 'Tha's two full mixed grills, two fish an' chips, one traybake with custard, one roly-poly with custard an' ice cream, an' two Tart Citrons. There's a bit of a wait but I'll push them through as quickly as I can.'

In spite of having their leisurely lunch broadsided, Hettie decided to use the situation to her advantage. It was a gift to have two principal members of the Catberry family on her own turf without the constraints that clearly existed at the family's home under the watchful eye of Praline and her daughters. As they waited for their lunches to arrive, it seemed the perfect moment to ask a few questions.

'Your grandmother has asked to see us on Monday,' said Hettie, 'which is a bit of a surprise, as we didn't think she approved of us being brought in to investigate. Do you know why she might have changed her mind?'

'Probably because of the row that kicked off at breakfast this morning,' said Grace. 'After she announced that she was closing the factory, things got even nastier than last night. Pops said he was resigning and going away with Morgana. Oliver and Rhubarb said they were happy to take over from him, saying they could do a better job between them, at which point we crept out before we got involved in the crossfire.'

'What about Lolly and Morgana? Did they have anything to say?'

Grace shook her head. 'No, neither of them was at breakfast. They're probably licking their wounds from last night.'

'And do you think your father will leave the business?' asked Hettie.

The two sisters thought for a moment before Dandy replied. 'I think he feels really hurt. He's worked so hard since Grandpa died to bring the family together and it's made things really difficult for him and Morgana. He loves her but I think he knows he's losing her, and with all this trouble over the bodies, things are just getting worse. He's been through so much bad stuff, having to come to terms with our mother's death and then Grandpa's. I think he might just decide to walk away.'

'I gather your mother's death was a tragic accident? That must have left a very big hole in your lives?' prompted Hettie.

Grace looked down at her DMs, suddenly silent, and Dandy struggled to find some words. 'We still can't believe it,' she said eventually, her eyes filling with tears. 'Such a stupid accident that no one could have predicted. Grandpa let us name a new chocolate bar after her – the Caramela Delight. It's a really big seller. I'm doing Easter eggs in it this year. Grandpa had a real soft spot for our mother. I like to think that wherever they are now they're looking out for each other. We miss them both desperately.'

'The trouble is, Grandpa glued us all together,' added Grace. 'He was so much fun. He had a wicked twinkle about him that could defuse any argument. He loved his family and his business and we were all happy to dance around him. Since our mother and he died, things just haven't been the same and Granny seems angry all the time.'

'You mentioned that your grandpa took a fancy to Morgana and welcomed her into the family,' said Hettie. 'That must have been awkward for your grandmother and your father.'

'There was nothing meant by it,' said Grace. 'Grandpa had an eye for a good-looking female but Morgana is not the sort of wife that Granny wanted for Pops. She loved our mother and thought she would have gone on to run the business with Pops, but after she died no one would have ever been good enough to replace her. Morgana is a blatant fortune hunter and doesn't try to hide it, which is why the rest of the family hate her – because she's not one of us.'

'Do you both hate her?'

Dandy shook her head. 'No, actually. I quite admire her. It takes a lot of guts to be an outsider in our family and she did make Pops happy until Grandpa died.'

'She's actually quite interesting when you get to know her,' said Grace. 'She's never shown any interest in the factory but she produced and directed several plays for our theatre group and got us to do the music, and she used to help out with the activities at Sunny Tails, the workers' retirement home in the village. When Grandpa died and Pops had to step up in his place, she just lost interest in everything. She sits around reading Agatha Crispys and Doris L. Slayer books these days.'

'We actually know Miss Crispy quite well,' said Tilly. 'We've worked on a couple of cases with her, at her London home and in Devon.'

'That is sooo cooool,' said the sisters in unison. 'What's she like?' asked Dandy.

'Just like anyone's favourite granny, but with an incredible mind for murder,' said Tilly, getting into her subject before Molly Bloom interrupted the flow by delivering two mixed grills, followed by Dolly with the fish and chips.

The four cats tucked into their lunches, suspending all meaningful discussion until their plates were licked clean. Hettie was pleased with how the conversation had been going but still had more questions, knowing that she must now prepare herself for the meeting with Praline Catberry on Monday. 'Tell me about Oliver and Rhubarb,' she began, as Dolly swept the plates away. 'Oliver seems to be a hard-working, safe pair of paws. Has he been managing the factory for long?'

'Grandpa took him on as an apprentice when he was barely more than a kitten,' said Dandy. 'He worked his way up, doing every job until he knew that factory like the back of his paw, so after he'd declared himself to Aunty Rhubarb it was a foregone conclusion that he would become management. He runs that place like clockwork.'

'And what about Rhubarb? Where does she sit in the scheme of things?'

'She is Queen of biscuits,' said Grace, 'and tenaciously guards her position as if her life depended on it. The biscuits do well but we're in direct competition with McKitties, which can make things difficult at times.'

'In what way?' asked Hettie.

'Well, the Catberrys and the McKitties have been feuding over their products since our great-grandfather Sylvester's time. The last run-in was over the annual darts match, which created a load of bad feeling. Granny is of the opinion that we should get out of biscuits altogether and produce more chocolate lines,' said Grace, as Molly Bloom delivered the puddings, 'but Rhubarb has dug her heels in as it's the only part of the business that's hers. Grandpa left it to her.'

Once again, the four cats focused on their food but Hettie was keen not to lose the thread of conversation and the Catberry sisters seemed happy to answer anything she raised with them. 'What happens to your inheritance if your father decides to leave the business?' she asked, through a mouthful of traybake and custard.

'We're next in line but I suppose it will be up to Granny,' said Dandy. 'Oliver is keen to take over the whole thing with Rhubarb but I don't think Granny would stand for that. I just hope Pops changes his mind and stays on.'

'How would you two feel about having to run things?' asked Tilly. 'Wouldn't you have to give up your band?'

'That prospect is too awful to think about at the moment,' said Grace, 'just when we're breaking through. We've got enough responsibility as it is and it's difficult enough trying to balance it all. The thought of running the whole operation gives me the horrors but hopefully things will calm down and go back to normal, especially if you sort out these bodies so we can open the factory again.'

The conversation was halted for a few moments as Tilly's enthusiasm for her pudding spilt out across the table in a slick of ice cream and custard and the roly-poly pudding lived up to its name. With quick-thinking,

Hettie was able to recapture it before it hit the floor and she put it firmly back where it belonged. Dolly – ever watchful – arrived seconds later with a damp sponge to finish the job, leaving Tilly to clean herself up. Tilly loved her food and her food loved Tilly but sometimes during the course of a meal the unexpected would happen. Sauces of every kind were a particular hazard in her large paws, leaving her cardigans in the position of first defence. It was clear to Tilly that the Saturday cardigan she'd selected that morning had taken a serious hit and would now have to be relegated to the Butter sisters' twin-tub machine as soon as time allowed and the weather improved.

'Oliver told us that your Aunt Lolly used to work in the offices but had decided to retire to look after your grandmother? Was she happy to give her job up?' asked Hettie.

'More a case of having to,' said Dandy. 'She's always suffered with her nerves and she was making mistakes with the wages. She has what Granny calls dark moods, which didn't go down too well with the other cats in the office and at the factory. Granny sent her to Sunny Tails for some time out, but that just made her worse, so now she pretends to look after Granny – who doesn't need looking after at all, as you probably realised last night.'

'She certainly seemed quite formidable,' said Hettie. 'Thank you both for talking us through your family. It's been really helpful to try and understand where everyone sits and how they feel about each other. We've now got to try and get to the bottom of who the bodies belong to and why they were put into the chocolate, but sadly we feel it must be an inside job.'

'How exciting,' said Grace. 'So do you think we might have a murderer in the family?'

'I'm afraid I do,' said Hettie, 'but it's early days and there's a lot of work for Tilly and me to do. I'm just hoping that the rest of the family will be as candid as you both are.'

Dandy looked at her overlarge black watch, which had a spider that crawled around the numerals. 'Come on, Sis – we'd better start making tracks. Johnny wants us for a soundcheck at four before they open and we'll have to help get the gear out of the van.'

Hettie smiled to herself, remembering her music days and how relentless it was to keep a band on the road. The setting up and taking down, the highs and lows all suffered for the art, and the rare rewards that seemed to make it all worthwhile. As the two sisters paid up and went on their way, she found herself actually looking forward to the Gums and Noses gig at the Cat and Fiddle. 'I think we've left it a bit late to go to Jessie's today,' she said, 'and I'm keen to get a photo of that dead ginger cat from Morbid before we go back to Catberry Manor on Monday so shall we have a walk to Shroud and Trestle?'

'That's fine with me,' said Tilly, 'especially as we're going out for a treat later. It's been ages since we went to a proper gig – not since the Magical Mystery Paws Tour.'

'Let's just hope that tonight's gig doesn't turn out to be the carnage that that one was,' said Hettie sagely as they stepped out into the rain.

Chapter Thirteen

The Cat and Fiddle was packed to the rafters by the time Bruiser pulled Miss Scarlet up in the pub's car park, allowing Dolly to hop off the back of the bike and Hettie and Tilly to clamber out of the sidecar. Grace and Dandy had proved good to their word and left Hettie's name on the door, plus three guests. Inside there was a real buzz of expectation. The Gums and Noses fans had dressed in their finest Goth outfits, mimicking their music heroes with a multitude of pierced ears and noses, black bodices, satanic capes and an extraordinary collection of black leather and lace. Bruiser and Dolly blended in in their biker jackets but Hettie and Tilly felt a little out of place in their business macs.

All was well once they'd abandoned the coats, as Tilly had chosen a cardigan she rarely wore with a dancing skeleton on the back and Hettie had gone for a long-sleeved black T-shirt she'd bought years ago at a thrash metal convention, depicting a cat skull with red eyes. 'I'm feeling slightly older than I should for this sort of thing,' said Hettie as she stood at the bar, waiting to be served. 'What would you like to drink?'

Tilly thought for a moment, looking around her. 'I think I'll have a glass of ginger beer and a packet of salt and vinegar crisps.'

'You'll be lucky to get a glass of anything,' shouted Hettie over the noise of the crowd. 'They're only doing bottles – no room for social graces tonight, and no crisps. It's a case of stand up and sip up.'

'Well then, I'll have a bottle of Vimto,' said Tilly, being slowly crushed by two rather overbearing vampires with light-up fangs.

'Did you see where Bruiser and Dolly went?' shouted Hettie. 'I don't know whether to get them a drink or not.'

'I think they went straight to the front of the stage to get us a good place,' said Tilly, shaking herself free of the vampires.

Hettie decided on three bottles of cider and the Vimto and forced her way back into the throng, with Tilly fighting her way through behind her. They both headed for the front, where Bruiser and Dolly were taking up as much room as possible, waiting for them. Seconds later, Johnny Clash climbed up onto the stage to introduce the band, bashing one of the cymbals on the drum kit to get everyone's attention. 'Here's a band who'll get yer crucifix swingin' and yer piercings poppin'! Please put your paws together for Gums and Noses!'

The crowd roared as Grace Slink, Dandy Nosepeg, Crusty Catsick and Foxglove Nipton took to the stage. Foxglove dived onto her drum kit and started beating out an almost tribal rhythm, instantly taken up by the audience, who clapped along. Crusty added a pulsing bass line before Grace joined them with a screaming guitar riff, leaning into her speaker to create maximum feedback and then Dandy grabbed the microphone off its stand and began to chant into it, mesmerising those lucky enough to see what was happening on the stage.

Tilly stared with her mouth open at the spectacle and found it hard to believe that only a few hours ago they had been sitting with Grace and Dandy, having a normal lunch at Bloomers. Now the two Catberry sisters were cavorting around the stage in full Goth regalia, stamping out their unique interpretations of death rock and darkwave music, as if they'd just awoken from the tombs of the long dead. It was very hard to imagine them doing anything as mundane as making chocolate Easter eggs.

The band's assault on the audience was relentless with no time for introductions between songs, just a continuous stream of pulsating raw energy coming off every member of the girl Goth collective. Hettie was impressed – and it took a great deal to impress Hettie. She had strong feelings about bands who slopped on stage and disappeared into their own machine heads, caring little about entertaining an audience. She had always believed in stage craft and as she watched Gums and Noses she was completely convinced that they had that ability in spades. The sound was unique, new and innovative and there wasn't a cat in the audience who would disagree with her.

The interval came soon enough and this time Bruiser and Dolly fought their way to the bar for another round of drinks. The room began to clear, as many of the audience members went out into the car park for some fresh air.

'Well, if they don't get that support tour with the Travelling Whoopsies, there's no justice,' said Hettie, 'although if I were the Whoopsies manager, I'd be concerned about being upstaged.'

'They really are very good, aren't they?' said Tilly. 'Quite frightening in a way. I'm glad we know them. It seems such a waste, them being stuck in the chocolate factory.'

'I agree,' said Hettie, 'but they've got a job for life there and the music business carries no guarantees. You're only as good as the current trend. One minute everyone wants a piece of you and the next you're being spat out as a has-been or taken for a ride by dodgy management, who grab your money and run. I just hope that Johnny Clash knows what he's doing.'

'Hello, you two,' said a voice from behind them. 'Enjoying yourselves?'

'Morbid!' said Hettie. 'This is an unexpected pleasure. I thought you were going to be too busy to come down here this evening?'

'Mr Trestle gave me the night off at the last minute, so as you said you were going to be here when you popped in earlier, I thought I'd come and see the band and bring you those photos you wanted. I thought it would save you another trip before your meeting on Monday.'

'That's really kind,' said Hettie, taking the envelope that Morbid offered. 'Can we get you a drink? Bruiser and Dolly are at the bar.'

'No, I'm good – one cider is my limit. I'm strictly still on call and it wouldn't do to turn up to a removal three winding sheets to the wind.'

Tilly giggled. She loved Morbid's dry sense of humour, which seemed to her to be so much cleverer than the average silly joke. 'What do you think to the band?' asked Hettie.

'Totally mind-blowing,' said Morbid. 'They should be playing places much bigger than this. There's hardly room to lay a corpse out in here.'

Tilly giggled again as Dolly and Bruiser returned with the drinks. The room began to fill up and once again Johnny Clash brought the band back on stage for another electrifying set.

The five friends clapped and stamped as Gums and Noses went into orbit once again, with Dandy and Grace tearing into the set list like savage harpies, disturbing and confident in their delivery. All about them hung the symbols of death, a macabre pantomime of fashion – but before the night was over they would face the stark reality of what it really meant to have a life stolen away in the most cruel and vicious of circumstances.

Chapter Fourteen

Morgana stared up at the tall factory chimneys that stood like Goliaths against the night sky and shivered. She pulled her shawl about her, mourning the life she had so stupidly given up and the life that had given her up. Every day brought her more misery, more broken promises and a feeling that she was no longer in charge of her own destiny. She'd been sucked in to an existence that should have brought her joy; manipulated into thinking that she was wanted – loved, even – but now there was nothing; no reason to wake in the morning, no destination to reach by the end of the day. She had no choice but to make the best of it.

The noise behind her made her jump. She turned, raising her paw in recognition, but the blow was unexpected, the pain brief as she fell to the ground. She woke to the sound of pathetic mewing and tried to focus, realising that the sound was coming from her own throat. There was a taste of blood in her mouth and a blinding pain in her head. She had no recollection of what had gone before, just a feeling of her whole body being dragged along the wet ground. Her limbs had been bound and she struggled before another blow silenced her.

She prayed for oblivion but there was now a noise that grew louder and louder. Then the heat, welcome at first but hotter and hotter as the suffocating film covered her face. The more she breathed, the tighter it became, until – eventually – she was grateful that it was over.

Chapter Fifteen

The evening had gone well for Gums and Noses. With three encores still ringing in their fans' ears, the band finally left the stage and the audience made its way home. The gig had overrun but the land-lord rubbed his paws together; pleased with his bar takings, he turned a blind eye to how late it was, showing a blatant disregard for those cats who lived in close proximity to his pub and liked to be in bed by eleven.

By the time Hettie and Tilly clambered into the side-car, it was ten minutes past midnight. Bruiser kicked the bike into life and sped off, with Dolly hanging on to him. All four cats were hungry and hoped that Greasy Tom's mobile takeaway van would still be serv-ing outside St Kipper's.

'Looks like we're in luck,' shouted Hettie above the roar of Miss Scarlet's engine, as Bruiser swung the bike into the high street and applied the brakes outside the church. 'What do you fancy? My shout and I'm going for the giant sausage dog.'

'I'd like a kebab for a change,' said Tilly, pulling the lid back on the sidecar, 'but I don't want much of that cabbage stuff in it.'

Bruiser and Dolly were already at Tom's van by the time Hettie joined them, leaving Tilly waiting patiently in Miss Scarlet for her supper. The rain had finally stopped and she was enjoying the night air after the heat and noise of the Cat and Fiddle.

Dolly and Bruiser had both chosen double whopper burgers and Tilly elected to keep them safe as Bruiser drove up the high street, dropping Hettie and Tilly off at the bakery before taking Dolly back to eat her supper in his shed, where he had a nice bottle of fiery ginger beer to share with her. Bruiser and Dolly had been walking out together for some time and suited each other very well. Both had a passion for motorbikes, leathers and food and – if pressed – Bruiser would have to admit that Dolly Scollop was the love of his life.

Hettie and Tilly crept in through the back door and into their room, doing their best not to wake Betty and Beryl in their flat upstairs. Tilly put the kettle on to make two mugs of milky tea as Hettie coaxed the fire back to life, adding some sticks to the embers that still glowed from earlier. 'I hope Grace and Dandy get to go on the Travelling Whoopsies tour,' said Hettie, settling down in her armchair with her giant hot dog sausage. 'They should take some time out from that chocolate factory and follow their dream.'

Tilly delivered a mug of tea to the arm of Hettie's chair before taking her own tea and kebab to her blanket. 'It sounds to me like there might not be a chocolate factory for much longer,' she said. 'The whole family seems to be at war and then there's the not-so-small problem of the bodies in The Tabby in Black chocolates. I wonder if Pettifur managed to get them recalled before he decided to quit the job?'

'Well, I suppose everything should be clearer after our audience with Praline Catberry on Monday,' said Hettie. 'Maybe she'll have patched things up with Pettifur by then.'

'I don't know why I don't have a Greasy Tom kebab more often,' said Tilly, changing the subject. 'It's not as messy as a hot dog or a burger.'

Hettie smiled at her friend. 'You could make a plain slice of bread messy without trying, but the main thing is that you enjoy your food – and we were lucky to find Greasy Tom's still open.'

The two cats finished their suppers and settled down for the night. An hour later, the phone in the staff sideboard began to ring. Tilly staggered out of her blanket, still with her eyes closed, and forced her way into the sideboard, fighting the cushions as she went to answer the call while Hettie sat up and rubbed her eyes. 'The No. 2 Feline Det—' she said, then was cut off in mid-sentence by the caller at the other end. She listened intently before responding. 'Oh dear,' she said. 'We'll do our best, but it is the middle of the night. The main thing is not to touch anything and we'll be with you as soon as we can.' She replaced the receiver and pushed the phone unceremoniously back into the sideboard.

'Well?' said Hettie, seeing the look of shock on Tilly's face.

'It was Pettifur Catberry,' said Tilly. 'Morgana has been shrink-wrapped at the factory.'

'What?!' said Hettie. 'Is she dead?'

'Yes,' said Tilly. 'Very dead by the sound of it. Pettifur wants us to go out there now. He's in bits.'

'Bloody marvellous,' said Hettie. 'Why cats can't be murdered in daylight I'll never know. I assume she was murdered?'

'I think that's for us to decide,' said Tilly, pulling on her cardigan. 'Shall I go and wake Bruiser while you get dressed?'

'I suppose so,' said Hettie. 'The sooner we get there and see what's happened, the sooner we can come back to bed.'

Tilly let herself out of the back door and made her way down the garden to Bruiser's shed. Luckily he was awake, as he'd only just returned from walking Dolly back to her flat above Bloomers. He answered Tilly's knock straight away. 'We think Morgana Catberry has been murdered,' she said. 'In fact, according to Pettifur, she's been shrink-wrapped.'

'Blimey!' exclaimed Bruiser. 'Them Catberrys don't do things by 'arves. What an awful way ta go. I'll stick on me leathers an' see you both out front with Miss Scarlet.'

Tilly returned to Hettie, who was dressed and ready to leave. She grabbed her notepad and pushed it into her satchel and the two cats made their way down the side of the bakery and out into the high street. Minutes later they were on their way to Catberry-on-the-Brink.

Catberry Manor was ablaze with lights as Bruiser drove up the driveway, standing out like a giant battle-ship against the night sky. It was Pettifur who loomed into view as they parked the motorbike. He gave the appearance of an escaped lunatic, weaving from side to side and muttering to himself as Hettie and Tilly jumped out of the sidecar and approached him.

Dandy and Grace stood on the steps, looking con-cerned for him and huddled in their dressing gowns. Behind them the rest of the Catberrys stood in the open doorway, all wearing their night clothes. Framed against the backdrop of the Manor House, they looked like the cast of one of Miss Crispy's thrillers. It instantly reminded Hettie of the photograph taken at Horace Catberry's funeral. The only cat fully dressed was Pettifur.

'You must come to the factory,' Pettifur said, digging his claws into the sleeve of Hettie's mac. 'It's awful! How could anyone do this to her? I was going to take her away from all this so that we could be happy, but now we'll never be happy.'

Pettifur continued to ramble and sob as Hettie led him to Miss Scarlet and forced him into the sidecar. Tilly squeezed in beside him as Hettie clambered up behind Bruiser and the four cats left the Manor behind, taking the road to the factory. As they pulled up in the car park, the night watch cat emerged from his shelter by the doors to the loading bay and came towards them. Hettie helped Pettifur out of the sidecar, swiftly followed by Tilly.

Hettie noticed that the watch cat was staggering slightly and, as he reached them, she could smell beer on his breath. It was obvious that he was drunk and when he spoke his words were slurred. 'I never seen no one, Mr Pettifur,' he said. ''Onest – no one gets past me.'

Pettifur brushed him aside and made for the entrance, followed by Hettie, Tilly and Bruiser. Once they were inside, Pettifur closed the doors. The loading bay was in darkness and he reached for the light switches. Suddenly the factory came to life as the long strip lights in the roof flickered and became static, illuminating two large lorries and a fleet of Creamy Egg cars, currently redundant but ready to spring into action once the factory reopened.

Pettifur faltered for a moment, pausing at the double doors that led into the production areas, but Bruiser – who'd had the benefit of a guided tour – went ahead of him, leading Hettie and Tilly towards the giant shrink-wrap machine. On first sight, it resembled a long tunnel where boxes of chocolates were fed in one end and emerged at the other, heat-sealed in a fine but durable polythene and ready for loading onto pallets.

There was no doubt that it was an ingenious way of protecting the products from any form of tampering, but as Hettie stared down at the dead cat in front of her, she found it hard to believe that anyone could be that cruel. Morgana was only just recognisable, her face contorted and her mouth wide open where she'd gasped for breath, making things worse as she'd inhaled the polythene which had eventually smothered her. The rest of her body was tightly wrapped as if she were cocooned, but there was little doubt that – try as she might – there would have been no escape. Whoever had done this to her had wanted her out of the way for good and had possibly delighted in the actual murder itself.

'This is a bad one,' said Hettie, taking a closer look at the body lying on the rollers. 'Whoever did this wanted her death to have the maximum impact on whoever found her.'

'And she must 'ave suffered,' said Bruiser. 'I watched 'em shovin' stuff through and when it comes out it's too 'ot ta touch. The cat doin' it Fridee 'ad ta wear oven gloves so she didn't burn 'er paws.'

'What a horrible way to die,' said Hettie taking a closer look at the body, 'the state of her suggests she was alive when she was fed into the machine.'

Tilly glanced only briefly at the body, then retreated back to the double doors where Pettifur was standing frozen to the spot. She tried to comfort him but he just stared straight ahead, suddenly disconnected from the scene before him.

'We'd better get Morbid on this straight away,' said Hettie. 'We'll leave everything as it is and go back to the Manor to call her. Then we'll have to establish where everyone was this evening and who saw Morgana last and when. She didn't turn up for breakfast this morning so this might have happened much earlier in the day, or even Friday night after the fight at dinner. I'll have to speak to Pettifur first.'

Hettie looked across at the cat who had been plunged into abject misery, knowing that her investigations would make his grief much worse before it got better. She would now have to open wounds in the Catberry family until the truth finally bled out.

Chapter Sixteen

By the time Bruiser had driven Hettie, Tilly and Pettifur back to the Manor, Sparks had gathered the family together in the day room, where he'd lit a fire. He'd woken the maid and instructed her to cut fresh sandwiches and heat up some soup. It was four o'clock and still dark but the birds were in full voice as they summoned up their dawn chorus, keen to start another day.

Bruiser and Tilly escorted Pettifur to the day room to join the rest of his family. Hettie used the phone in the hallway to call Morbid. It took some time for her to answer but she promised to be at the factory within the hour with her van. Hettie suggested that Bruiser would meet her and take her to the body. Having organised the removal, Hettie made her way into the day room. The family sat on various chairs and sofas in silence as she entered; only Pettifur was on his feet, pacing in front of the fire. Tilly and Bruiser stood by the door and Hettie discreetly asked Bruiser to return to the factory to meet up with Morbid before addressing the family.

'I assume that you're all aware by now that Morgana has been murdered,' she began. 'Pettifur has asked us to investigate her death and so I must ask you all to be as helpful as you can in allowing us to eliminate you from our enquiries. This means that we will talk to you one by one to establish your movements over the last twenty-four hours and to find out when it was you last saw Morgana.'

Praline, who'd been listening intently, offered a sudden angry outburst. 'This is ridiculous! Are you suggesting that one of us murdered Morgana?'

'I'm afraid that is the most likely explanation at the moment, which is why I need to gather the facts, establish strong alibis and explore possible motives until we get to the truth,' said Hettie.

'The truth is that I'm not sure I want my family invaded in such a way,' said Praline. 'As you witnessed last night, Morgana wasn't well liked in this family. She was a difficult cat to know but she made herself unpopular. I can't help but feel that whatever has befallen her is entirely her own fault.'

Hettie decided to risk being thrown off the case by hitting back at Praline. 'Her own fault, you say? I suggest you come with me now to view her body on the rollers of the shrink-wrap machine – trussed up in polythene, suffocated and having been put through the most unimaginable torture. If someone in this room has done that, then they are entirely capable of killing again – and next time it could be you or Grace or Dandy. Any of you.'

Praline stared at the floor, fidgeting with the top of her walking stick before lifting her head. 'Very well, please go about your business, but I wish to be kept up to date with all your enquiries and I will make any necessary decisions regarding the family. I will now return to my bed, but before I go I should point out that I have been in my rooms since leaving the orangery on Friday evening. Lolly has been with me for some of that time. I made a brief appearance at breakfast this morning to announce that the factory will be closed until further notice and I haven't seen Morgana since Friday evening. If you have any questions, I suggest you ask them at our meeting on Monday morning. I shall expect you at ten.'

Praline swept from the room, leaving the family to stare after her. The only cat who showed no reaction was Pettifur. He continued to pace up and down, seemingly unaware of anything and anyone around him. Sparks arrived with a tray full of sandwiches, followed by the maid carrying a large soup tureen, which she put down on a table. The Catberrys suddenly came to life, helping themselves to the food as if they hadn't eaten for a week. Only Pettifur resisted and Hettie decided that it was time to talk to him. She approached Sparks and asked if the library could be made available for interviews. He nodded and went to light a fire.

After the scrum for the food had died down, Hettie and Tilly helped themselves to moderate plates of salmon and cucumber sandwiches, knowing that it was probably going to be a very long time until breakfast. Sparks returned a few minutes later and nodded to Hettie, at which point Tilly took Pettifur by the arm and led him from the room towards the library.

'I'll need to talk to you and your brother at some stage,' said Hettie, as Sparks held the library door open for her, 'and perhaps the maid as well, but I'm keen to talk to the family first.'

'Very good,' said Sparks. 'I'll let them know and if you need anything else there's a bell pull by Mr Pettifur's desk.'

Sparks returned to his butler pantry as Hettie entered the library. The fire was very welcome and Tilly had persuaded Pettifur to sit by it. She sat next to him and Hettie pulled another chair up to sit opposite. 'I know this is a terrible time for you,' Hettie began, 'but we need to understand what has happened here and to do that I need your help.'

Pettifur looked up and slowly nodded. Tilly pulled her notepad and pencil from her satchel and wrote 'Pettifur' at the top of a clean page as Hettie asked her first question. 'When did you last see Morgana?'

'This morning, before I went down to breakfast,' said Pettifur. 'She said she felt unwell after her fight with Lolly and that she was going to spend the day in her room reading.'

'So you didn't see her later at supper?'

'No. I called in to see if she was coming down to dinner at around seven, but she wasn't in her room. I'd been out at the factory all day, closing it all down with Oliver after Mother insisted. We had a row about it at breakfast and I told them I'd had enough and wanted to leave the business. When I went to find Morgana, I was going to tell her that I'd resigned and that we should go away together and start a new life.'

Pettifur faltered for a moment or two and Hettie waited before asking her next question. 'You say she wasn't in her room at seven last night – have you any idea where she might have gone?'

Pettifur shook his head. 'No, but it wasn't unusual for her to take a walk before dinner. She often walked through the village up to Sunny Tails, our retirement home. She used to help out there.'

'And what about later, when you went to bed – did you see her then?'

'No. We have separate rooms as she's such a light sleeper and I often work late here in the library. I didn't go to bed. I spent last night going through some of my father's papers, looking at how easy it might be to leave the business and what I would be entitled to if I did.'

'And can anyone vouch for having seen you last night in the library?'

'Well, Dandy and Grace popped their heads round the door at about one o'clock to say they'd had a very good concert and to say goodnight, and Sparks brought me a drink after dinner at about ten o'clock.'

'You called us at around half past two to say that Morgana had been murdered at the factory – did you find her?'

Pettifur put his head down again, reliving the moment. 'Yes. The night watch cat called me to say that the shrink-wrap machine was still switched on when he was doing his rounds and that the doors to the production area were open. I thought we might have had a break-in so I walked to the factory and that's when I found her.'

'What did you do at that point?'

'I switched the machine off and shook her, hoping that she might still be alive, but the film was so tightly bound around her that I knew it was no good. She was barely recognisable. I'm not entirely sure what I did after that. I remember screaming at the night watch cat, blaming him for what had happened, and he admitted that he'd slept through most of the evening, but I could see that he was drunk. Somehow, I got back to the Manor and called you.'

'What did you do after you called us?'

'I woke my mother and went to tell Grace and Dandy in their rooms. They woke the rest of the family and we all waited for you to arrive.'

'Did you tell the family what had happened to Morgana?'

'I think I did. To be honest, I don't know what I said. I just kept thinking about her body in that machine and how she must have suffered. And it was all my fault.'

'Why do you say that?'

'Because I should have stuck up for her more with my mother and my sisters after my father died. I know they treated her badly, making her feel like an outsider. My father had a soft spot for her and welcomed her into the family like one of his own daughters, and I don't think that went down very well with Lolly and Rhubarb, but after he died they could hardly stand to be in the same room as her without starting an argument or a fight.'

'And what about your mother? What did she have against Morgana?'

'She loved Caramela, my first wife, and never accepted Morgana. She said she was a troublemaker and a fortune hunter.'

'Oliver seems to be very much part of the family. How did he get on with Morgana?'

'I think he liked her, but Rhubarb rules the roost there. She never liked him getting too close to Morgana. Oliver is a good manager but he's never learnt to manage Rhubarb, who is a law unto herself. She's even been known to win arguments with my mother.'

'Like the biscuits?' Hettie suggested.

Pettifur looked surprised for a moment before responding. 'Yes. Mother wants us out of biscuits but my father cleverly left that part of the business entirely to Rhubarb and no one can change that.'

'Did he leave anything in particular to your sister Lolly?'

'She has a share in Sunny Tails but he left a bigger share to Morgana and I've no idea what will happen to that now. I suppose it will come to me.'

'What exactly is Sunny Tails for?' asked Hettie.

'It was started by my grandfather Sylvester for the workers who had to retire through old age or sickness. He believed in looking after all the cats he employed. Sunny Tails is a substantial house in the centre of the village, with beautiful gardens and plenty of activities for the older cats to enjoy. Morgana loved going there to help out. She ran drama groups and did hair and make-up sessions for the residents. I think that's why my father gave her shares – she did so much good there. After he died, she seemed to lose interest, but she loved the gardens and still enjoyed walking round them. That's where I thought she'd gone last night.'

Pettifur crumpled and became distraught and Hettie decided to bring the interview to a close. The cat in front of her was clearly exhausted and she doubted he could be much more help under the circumstances. She stood up and crossed to Pettifur's desk, where she pulled the bell rope. Sparks responded within minutes. 'Mr Pettifur needs some rest,' she said. 'I think you should take him to his room, then ask Miss Lolly Catberry to join us here in the library.'

Sparks nodded and helped his master to the door, but Pettifur turned before he was led away. 'Morgana,' he said. 'What will happen to her? She won't just stay like that, will she?'

'I assure you she's in safe paws,' said Hettie. 'Our good friend Morbid is looking after her and I'm sure you'll be able to visit her in a few days to see Morgana as you remember her and not as you found her tonight.'

'Thank you,' said Pettifur, as Sparks gently led him out of the library.

'Poor cat,' said Tilly after the door had closed.

'Who do you mean?' said Hettie. 'Pettifur or Morgana?'

'Both, I suppose,' said Tilly, 'but Pettifur is the one left behind and there doesn't seem to be anyone he can share his grief with except maybe Dandy and Grace. They seem to be the only ones who actually liked Morgana.'

'And they're the only members of the family who have an alibi, as we were with them all evening at the Cat and Fiddle – unless they shrink-wrapped their stepmother as they were getting home from their gig, which I think is highly unlikely. I'd put money on the rest of the family telling us that they were all in bed by ten. The difficult bit for us is breaking down those alibis. I'm certain they'll all stick together and surprisingly they all seem to have a motive for wanting Morgana out of the way. I think her very presence in this family ruffled the fur sufficiently for one of them to take extreme action but that cat is cruel, calculating and vicious – and, I suspect, very clever at hiding it.'

Chapter Seventeen

Lolly Catberry gave every impression that she was a cat who lived on her nerves. When Sparks delivered her to the library, she stood timidly at the door as if she wasn't allowed any further into the room. Hettie beckoned her to the seat that Pettifur had just given up, offering a reassuring smile as Tilly turned to a clean page in her notepad. The scratches from Lolly's fight with Morgana were still raw and visible and Hettie thought that was a good place to start. 'You obviously didn't get on with Morgana,' she said. 'Was there any particular reason for the fight on Friday night?'

'I was defending my mother,' said Lolly. 'Since my father's death, Morgana has been trying to push my mother out so that she could run things her way. She's been trying to get her to move to Sunny Tails so that she could lord it over the rest of us here at the Manor and Pettifur just stood back and let her. After she slapped me, I thought it was time to teach her a lesson.'

'And now Morgana is dead, how do you feel about her?'

'I don't feel anything for her,' said Lolly. 'I just hope that now she's gone we can all get back to being family again.'

'When did you last see Morgana?'

'On Friday night in the dining room with a joint of beef on her head. Rhubarb and Oliver left with me and Rhubarb came to my room to bathe my injuries. I didn't see or hear Morgana after that, as her rooms are on the other side of the house.'

'And what did you do on Saturday?'

'I was sore from the fight so I had my breakfast in bed and stayed there until lunchtime, when I visited my mother. She told me that Pettifur was thinking of resigning from the company because there had been a row at breakfast over closing the factory. We had a sandwich together in her sitting room, then I spent the afternoon with her. I went back to my room for the evening and Sparks brought my dinner up on a tray. I read my book for a while and fell asleep at about ten o'clock. The next thing I knew was Grace hammering on my bedroom door, telling me to get up as Morgana had been murdered. I went to my mother's room to collect her and we all assembled downstairs as you arrived.'

'So the only cats you saw yesterday were your mother, Sparks and later Grace and you didn't leave the Manor for any reason?'

'That's right,' said Lolly, a little too quickly. 'I really am quite tired so if there's nothing else I'd like to go to my room and rest.'

'Of course,' said Hettie, 'but before you go, it would be good to know a little more about you and where you fit into the family and the business.'

'I don't see how that can help you with Morgana's murder,' said Lolly. 'This is all so intrusive.'

'I'm afraid in the case of murder everyone's lives are laid open to scrutiny. With a family like yours and the position Morgana had in it, I wouldn't be doing my job if I didn't get some background on the cats I'm talking to. I gather you've retired from the business to look after your mother?'

'Yes, that's right. I got fed up with being in the office and arranging the occasional open day, and the factory never really interested me, so I decided to become my mother's companion after my father died.'

'I gather your father left shares in Sunny Tails to you and Morgana – that must have been difficult, as you weren't exactly friends,' suggested Hettie.

Lolly looked a little disturbed for a moment but recovered herself sufficiently to close the subject down. 'Yes, it was a surprise to us all that Morgana was left shares in Sunny Tails, especially as my father had always promised it to me. I expect to inherit all of it now, if Pettifur and my mother can agree. I suppose you're thinking that gives me a motive for murder, but to be honest I can't stand the place. If I do inherit it, I shall sell it and enjoy the money it brings.'

Hettie was a little surprised at Lolly's frankness but decided to probe further. 'Why don't you like the place? It seems a lovely idea to offer a retirement home to the factory workers in their old age?'

'I suppose it's because Morgana spent so much time there, changing and reorganising everything. I never got a look-in. I just didn't like the way the place was being run.'

'How do you get on with your sister, Rhubarb?' asked Hettie. 'Are you close?'

'Not very close,' said Lolly. 'Rhubarb is totally driven by her biscuits. There's not much room in her life for anything else – not even Oliver, really. She was always my father's favourite until Morgana came along. Poor Pettifur fell hook, line and sinker for Morgana's charms but he didn't notice how close she was to my father.'

'Was that a problem?'

'Not any more, now they're both dead,' said Lolly. 'Now, if you'll excuse me, I need to go to my room. I'm starting a headache.'

'Before you do, would you take a look at this photograph?' said Hettie, as Tilly scrabbled in her satchel for the envelope that Morbid had given them. 'I'm afraid it's of one of the dead cats we found in the chocolate vat. I wonder if you recognise her?'

Lolly gave the photograph a cursory glance before shrugging her shoulders. 'No, I've never seen that cat before. Now I must go and lie down.'

This time Lolly gave Hettie no opportunity to ask any more questions. She stood and walked to the door, closing it behind her. 'Well, that was enlightening,' said Hettie, getting up to pull the bell rope. 'I suspect there was no love lost between Lolly and her father and Morgana definitely wasn't numbered amongst her friends. I'm sure she recognised the ginger cat in the photo though.'

'I've started a suspects list,' said Tilly. 'I've put Lolly at the top of it for now. Shall I put Pettifur on it too?'

'Why not?' said Hettie, warming her paws on the fire. 'As far as I can see, the field's wide open for Morgana's murder as no one seemed to get on with her. I imagine she'd even become a problem to Pettifur after his father died and there's a mystery in itself. I still don't believe the Mog Nob choking story – and for that matter, Pettifur's first wife's death is odd too. The TV would pay big money for a saga based on the Catberrys.'

Sparks interrupted Hettie's train of thought by arriving with a tray of sandwiches and a pot of tea. 'I thought you might like something before your next interview,' he said, putting the tray down on a table next to the fire.

'Thank you,' said Hettie, suddenly realising how hungry she was. It was five o'clock on Sunday morning, and normally she wouldn't be awake for another six hours. 'I'd like to speak to Mrs Rhubarb Crumbwell next.'

Sparks nodded and left the library, allowing Hettie and Tilly to pounce on the sandwiches, washing them down with cups of milky tea.

Chapter Eighteen

Rhubarb Crumbwell was nothing like her sister Lolly. She walked into the library with a very confident air about her, her head held high, and every bit Praline's daughter. She avoided the chair that Hettie offered her and pulled up one of her choice from behind Pettifur's desk. High-backed, it gave her a certain amount of authority over Hettie and Tilly, who were sitting in the more comfortable armchairs.

'I'm sorry to keep you up so late,' said Hettie, 'but we're trying to establish Morgana's last movements so that we can build a picture of what happened to her.'

'I'm surprised anyone cares,' said Rhubarb. 'She's been nothing but trouble since Pettifur brought her home to tea, and so soon after Caramela's death. He should be ashamed of himself for subjecting us to her. She should have married the McKittie's heir instead of training her sights on Pettifur. My brother is easily led. He's good with business but his personal life is a desert of fear and uncertainty. As the heir, he was raised to take on responsibility and with Caramela by his side it worked, but after she died I think he lost his way.'

Hettie was beginning to feel that her interview was being hijacked. She decided to turn the conversation away from Pettifur, bringing the focus back to Morgana's murder. 'When did you last see Morgana?'

'About eight o'clock last night,' said Rhubarb. 'I was watching TV in the day room and I got up to close the curtains and saw her walking down the drive towards the village.'

'And were you on your own in the day room?'

'If you mean can anyone corroborate where I was, then my answer is no. I'd taken a tray in my room for supper at seven, then I came down to watch some TV before bed. They were showing *The African Queen* with Katherine Catburn, my favourite actress. I watched the film and went to bed around ten. I woke up as Dandy was shouting at my door, saying Morgana had been murdered. I shook Oliver awake and we came downstairs together.'

'If you watched the film on your own, where was Oliver at that time?'

'Well, I don't think he was murdering Morgana, if that's what you mean. He said he was going to play cards with Perks in his flat over the garages. He's our chauffeur cum odd-job cat, Sparks's brother. Oliver and Perks are seasoned gamblers and have a lot in common as they both started here as kittens.'

'And what time did Oliver come to bed?' asked Hettie.

'He was in bed and fast asleep by the time I went up. He'd been drinking for most of the day after the upset at breakfast.'

'Do you mean your mother closing the factory and Pettifur threatening to resign?'

'I'm impressed,' said Rhubarb sarcastically. 'It doesn't take you long to get under the skin of the Catberrys. Yes, he was very upset. He really cares about the chocolate business and does far more work than Pettifur. My father should have left the business to us but Pettifur was the first born and that is the family way.'

'He left you the biscuits, I gather?'

'Yes, that's right, and I've made a real go of it. If Oliver had been allowed to take over the chocolates, we'd have made a really good team.'

'Like your mother and father did?' suggested Hettie.

'I suppose so, although they were both living on past glories. My father changed very little about the business when he inherited it from my grandfather, like the old chocolate vats. He hated modernising. He should have changed them years ago, and my mother wanted to scale things down after he died and make the business more about chocolate and less about biscuits. I'm afraid that I won't let that happen, although these bodies in the old vat could wipe out the whole business if we don't get to the bottom of it.'

Hettie reached for the photo she'd shown Lolly and pushed it in front of Rhubarb's nose. 'On the subject of the bodies in the vat, do you recognise this cat?'

Rhubarb took the photo from Hettie for a closer look before dropping it and recoiling. 'Oh for pity's sake, that cat is dead, isn't it? I can't believe you're showing that around. It's indecent.'

'I'm sorry but it's easier than having you all troop down to the undertaker to look at her,' said Hettie. 'I'd appreciate it if you could take another look, just in case you recognise her.'

'No need,' said Rhubarb. 'I've seen enough to know that I've no idea who she is or was.'

'What can you tell me about the death of Pettifur's first wife?' asked Hettie.

Rhubarb looked slightly unsettled at the change of subject. 'Why do you ask?' she countered.

'Because her accident seems rather odd, in the same way as your father's death. Your family does seem rather accident-prone.'

'I'm not sure what you're getting at,' said Rhubarb indignantly. 'Are you suggesting that they were murdered too? Because if you are, you're being ridiculous. My father bolted his food as he grew older. We were always telling him to slow down. He even choked on a chicken bone at dinner once and Oliver had to save him. As for Caramela, she was just unlucky. That factory can be a killing machine at the best of times.'

'Especially the shrink-wrapper,' said Hettie, drily. 'Perhaps you'd be kind enough to ask Oliver to come and talk to us?'

Chapter Nineteen

Oliver Crumbwell looked like a cat with a sore head when he arrived in the library. He slumped down in the chair that Hettie offered him, showing no sign of the cat who had seemed so capable on Thursday when he had shown her the bodies in the vat. 'You look exhausted,' she said, trying the sympathetic approach as Tilly added Rhubarb to her suspects list and found a clean page. 'I can imagine how you feel about the factory being shut down.'

'It's not just that,' said Oliver. 'It just seems like one thing after another. I don't know what's happening in this family any more, or where I stand in it. Mr Horace would turn in his grave if he could see the mess we're in. I thought things were bad when I discovered those bodies in the old Tabby in Black vat but now Morgana has been murdered I don't know what to think.'

'Did you get on with Morgana?'

'I think I did,' said Oliver. 'To be honest, I felt sorry for her. She was a good-looking cat and that didn't go down well with Lolly and Rhubarb, but they had to put up and shut up when Mr Horace was alive. As soon as he died, the claws were out. She didn't stand a chance and poor old Pettifur stood back and let his sisters humiliate her and try to drive her out of the family.'

'Are you suggesting that Lolly and Rhubarb may have murdered Morgana?'

'Of course not,' protested Oliver. 'I just meant that after Mr Horace died, Morgana had no one to stick up for her and she didn't do herself any favours either. She was always having a go about how she hated the factory and wanted Pettifur to give up his inheritance. She said some pretty bad things about my mother-in-law too, as you witnessed on Friday at dinner. You take Praline on at your peril but Morgana wasn't a cat to hide her feelings. She was actually far more honest than the rest of us and I think that's what got her killed. It was always going to end in tears. Sadly, except for Pettifur, no one's crying for her now.'

'Tell me about yesterday,' said Hettie. 'How did you spend your time?'

'Ah, I suppose you're looking at alibis,' said Oliver, rubbing his paw across his head. 'I'm afraid I was very angry for most of yesterday after my mother-in-law announced that she was closing the factory. All our plans for the Easter products flew out of the window. As it was, we were up against it with only a couple of weeks before the Easter eggs had to be distributed to the shops. That's my job, to see that all the deadlines are met, but the rug was pulled from under me. And now we have a murder on our paws as well as the bodies in the vat, so I can't see us climbing out of this nightmare any time soon.'

'So what did you do yesterday?' pressed Hettie.

'I went over to the factory after breakfast with Pettifur and we sent all the staff home. We closed down all the machinery and made sure that everything was safe and locked up. Pettifur then went over to the office to catch up on some paperwork. I didn't feel like going back to the Manor so I walked into the village and had lunch at the Brink, our local pub. I stayed on there with some of the workers from the factory as the landlord decided to have a lock-in. I had too much to drink and met up with Perks, our chauffeur. He suggested I go back to his flat to sober up. He made cheese on toast and then we played poker until about nine o'clock. I began to feel better after all the drink so I left him to get some fresh air. I walked over to the factory. The night watch cat was asleep in his tin shed but I decided not to wake him and walked back to the Manor and put myself to bed.'

'And when did you last see Morgana?'

'On Friday night in the dining room, after the fight with Lolly.'

'And you didn't see her again last night – when you were getting some fresh air perhaps?'

Oliver held his head as if he was trying to remember something. 'I know it's strange but I thought I heard some machinery as I stood outside the factory. I knew I'd turned everything off, though, so I didn't bother to investigate. I thought it was probably the refrigeration unit kicking in. It's only just occurred to me that it could have been the shrink-wrap machine. Morgana could have been being murdered while I stood outside and did nothing.'

'You've been very helpful but just one more thing,' said Hettie, picking up the photo. 'This is a picture of the dead cat found in the chocolate vat. Morbid Balm thinks she died recently. Could you take a look?'

Oliver stared at the photo for some time before passing it back to Hettie and shaking his head. 'No, sorry. I've never seen that cat before.'

Chapter Twenty

Sparks arrived to put more coal on the library fire and Hettie decided that this would be the best time to talk to him. Like most butlers, he ran the house and his attention to detail was impressive, but Hettie decided to test his loyalty regarding the family. 'I gather from your brother Perks that your family has worked for the Catberrys for many years?' she said.

'That's right,' said Sparks. 'Our dad was the chauffeur and his brother, Uncle Ned, was butler to Mr Sylvester and Mr Horace until they both retired to Sunny Tails and we took over. They've both gone now, of course, but it was always expected that me and Perks would take on their jobs.'

'And do you enjoy your work?'

'Most of the time, although things have been quite difficult since Mr Horace passed on.'

'In what way?' asked Hettie, hoping that the butler would be indiscreet.

'Well, Mr Horace ruled the roost. He was a stickler for family traditions and insisted that everyone treated each other with respect. He gave all the family jobs to do and he expected them to do them well. He was a generous master to all of us but you never felt you could outwit him as he always seemed to be one step ahead, if you know what I mean.' Hettie nodded but allowed Sparks to continue. 'When he died, we were all naturally grief-stricken, but from that moment everything seemed to change. The family seem to be at each other's throats constantly. When they get together at meal times, there's always rows or even fights. Mr Pettifur seems powerless to stop it and the Mistress is just angry with everyone.'

'What about Morgana? Do you think she was to blame for the family falling out with each other?'

Sparks thought for a moment before replying. 'Miss Morgana certainly shook things up when Mr Pettifur brought her to the Manor, but in a good way. Grace and Dandy blossomed with their music and theatre because Miss Morgana encouraged them and Mr Horace was very pleased with the way she had taken to helping out at Sunny Tails. She did some good things there but the rest of the family was still missing Miss Caramela and didn't take to Miss Morgana at all. I think she was very lost after the master died. Mr Pettifur was too busy taking everything over to notice so she became quite sad and lost interest in everything.'

'When did you last see her?'

'I took up a breakfast tray to her rooms yesterday morning after Mr Pettifur told me she wasn't getting up. She seemed in a bad way after the fight with Miss Lolly. I sent the maid up to collect the tray later in the morning but it had been left outside her door untouched.'

'And you didn't see Morgana after that?'

Sparks shook his head. 'No, that was the last time I saw her. The trouble is you can go days in this house without seeing someone. Each member of the family has a suite of rooms and since Mr Horace died they spend more time in them. We're run ragged with the demand for trays in rooms, as they rarely eat together except on Fridays, when there's usually a row or a fight, and breakfasts.'

'Who did you serve trays to yesterday?' asked Hettie, keen to double check some of the alibis.

'Well, let me see,' said Sparks, scratching his head. 'The Mistress, Pettifur, Oliver and Miss Rhubarb all had breakfast together in the dining room. Miss Grace and Miss Dandy were there as well until the row began about closing the factory. I think they were pleased to have the day off, as they had a concert last night. They left to go into the town, I believe. I took a tray up to Miss Lolly, who was spending the morning in her room, and as I've just said, I took a tray to Miss Morgana.'

'What about later in the day?'

'I took a sandwich lunch up to the Mistress in her rooms, which she shared with Miss Lolly. Later I took supper trays to Miss Rhubarb and Miss Lolly at around seven and the Mistress rang for a late supper at around nine.'

'What about Pettifur?'

'He ate a cold meat salad in the dining room when he arrived back from the factory, then went to do some work here in the library, as he often does. I took him a drink at about ten o'clock before I went to bed.'

'Did you notice anything strange or out of the ordinary about anyone yesterday?'

'Well, obviously Miss Morgana and Miss Lolly were covered in scratches and bruises and I don't think I've ever seen Mr Pettifur so angry. After breakfast, he went up to the Mistress's rooms. I suppose he was trying to change her mind about closing the factory. I met him on the stairs after he'd seen her and he was in a blind rage. He seemed much calmer later, going through his papers in the library. I think he had decided to leave the Manor.'

'What makes you say that?' Hettie asked.

'He mentioned that he was thinking of refurbishing a house in the village that his father left him. He said he was too old to be living with his family and thought he might take up gardening.'

'Did that surprise you?'

'Not really. I think he thought that after Mr Horace died he would be able to run the business the way he wanted to and modernise everything, but the Mistress, Miss Rhubarb and Oliver were at odds with him, which I think he finds really frustrating. These bodies in the vat might be the final straw. I just don't know what will happen now he's lost Miss Morgana. I fear for him.'

Hettie was impressed with the empathy Sparks had shown his master but was keen to finish her interrogations as tiredness was beginning to engulf her. It had been a long night.

'Thank you for your time,' said Hettie. 'I think that concludes our interviews with the family for now, as we'll be speaking to your mistress on Monday, but we would like to have a word with your brother before we leave.'

'That's no problem,' said Sparks. 'He's here in the kitchens talking motorbikes with your driver. I saw him sitting out in his sidecar and fetched him in for a sandwich and a hot drink. Perks had come over from his flat when he saw all the lights on in the Manor. He thought someone had died – and he was right, of course.'

'It's very kind of you to look after Bruiser,' said Hettie. 'Perhaps you could let him know that we won't be much longer?'

Sparks left the library, giving Hettie and Tilly a few moments to come up for air. 'My head is spinning,' said Hettie. 'I hope you've got all this stuff down in your notebook so we can cross-reference it.'

'I think I have,' said Tilly. 'It seems to me that most of the Catberrys are quite nasty, especially to Morgana and poor Pettifur. They're all so jealous of each other, except for Grace and Dandy – they seem able to stay out of the worst of the family rows.'

'I suppose that's because they're young and their lives are in front of them,' said Hettie. 'I just wish we could have met Horace Catberry. He sounds like he was quite some cat. He'd have to have been to hold this family together but you do wonder why it's all fallen so badly apart since his death. You'd think Praline would be capable of playing the peacekeeper but from what I've seen she just seems to make things worse. She clearly has no faith in Pettifur running the company – or any of them, for that matter. I wonder what she'll have to say on Monday?'

Before Tilly could speculate, Sparks returned with his brother and a tray of coffees and Danish pastries. 'I'll leave you with Perks,' he said, putting the tray down and removing the earlier one. 'Miss Grace and Miss Dandy have asked if you wish to see them?'

'I think after speaking to your brother we'll go back to the town,' said Hettie. 'We'll have to call in at the undertakers and I think the family should get some rest. We're coming back on Monday so maybe we could speak to Grace and Dandy then if we need to?'

'Very good,' said Sparks. 'I'll let them know.'

Sparks left the library but his brother stood by the open doorway as if he were frightened to come any further into the room; the fact that he was wearing pyjamas and a dressing gown with his chauffeur's highly polished boots didn't help.

Hettie offered him a chair by the fire but Perks made it clear that he would rather stand. 'I think this is the first time I've been any further than the kitchens here at the Manor,' he said. 'It doesn't feel right being in the library.'

'I only have a few questions,' said Hettie, eyeing up the Danish pastries. 'I just wanted to check what you were doing yesterday and last night to see if we can piece the day together? Did you see Miss Morgana yesterday at any stage?'

Perks shook his head. 'No, I didn't, and what a terrible business. Your driver said she'd been shrink-wrapped. What a waste of such a beautiful cat and poor Mr Pettifur.'

'What did you do yesterday?' asked Hettie, avoiding getting too involved with Perks's thoughts on Morgana and the impact of her death.

'I changed the tyres round on the Rolls-Royce, which took most of the morning. I gave her a tune up, then later in the afternoon I took her out for a run through the village. I saw Mr Oliver outside the Brink, looking none too steady, so I suggested he come back with me to sober up. He told me he'd had to shut the factory and he was really upset. I think it was the drink talking, as he's usually a happy sort of fellow. I did cheese on toast for us, got some coffee down him and then we played poker and I sent him on his way just before nine. I listened to a play on the radio and turned in at about eleven. I woke up in the night thinking I hadn't locked the Rolls up so I went down to the garage to check and noticed all the lights on at the Manor. I came across to investigate and Sparks said that Miss Morgana had been found dead.'

'You seem to get on well with Oliver – do you regard him as a friend?'

'I suppose I do. We were virtually brought up together. He was an apprentice and I learnt my trade from my dad, who drove Mr Sylvester and Mr Horace after him. Oliver got lucky with Miss Rhubarb and became one of the family, rising up through the ranks to manager but he's never forgotten that him and me started out together and he confides in me.'

'In what way?' asked Hettie.

'Just male cat talk, that sort of thing. I think he finds it hard living with the family sometimes. He comes to me to get away from it all and we have a good laugh, although he always wins at cards.'

Hettie showed the photo of the ginger cat to Perks. 'Do you recognise her?' she said.

He scratched his ear as if he was trying to remember something. 'I can see that the poor thing is dead,' he said, 'but those markings on the top of her head are so familiar. I just can't think where I've seen them.'

'Thank you,' said Hettie. 'I think that's all for now but if you think of anything we should know or you can put a name to that photo, you can call us or we'll be back here on Monday.'

Perks had hardly shut the door behind him before Hettie and Tilly set about the Danish pastries, which were still warm. They made light work of them, washing them down with milky coffee. It was six in the morning and Hettie pulled open the heavy velvet curtains in the library to reveal the new day. In the distance, the giant chimneys of the chocolate factory rose up into the early dawn like symbols of all the Catberrys had achieved since the early days of Hauxston and Solomon. The family's journey had been interrupted along the way, like any other family, with power struggles, deaths and misfortunes – but it had also bred a killer capable of destroying everything their Victorian ancestors had worked so hard for.

'Come on,' said Hettie. 'Let's go and find Bruiser and go home. I think we've had more than enough of the Catberrys for one night.'

'Lovely,' said Tilly, packing her notepad away in her satchel, 'and look – the sun's coming up and it's actually stopped raining!'

Chapter Twenty-One

It was a glorious spring morning as Bruiser drove them back to the town. The sun shone down onto the puddles, making them look like pools of glass, and the hedgerows were alive with creatures going about their business, rejoicing in the better weather. It reminded Tilly of her favourite chapter in *The Wind in the Willows*, where Mole deserts his spring cleaning to go off and seek adventures. After the long and troublesome night, the early morning was a tonic to all three cats but they were still pleased to get back to their beds, if only for a few hours.

Hettie and Tilly slept through until Betty Butter knocked on their door at two o'clock in the afternoon. Tilly struggled from her blanket, not knowing what day it was, and opened the door to a tray of ham baps, crisps and freshly baked blueberry muffins.

'Sister and me thought you might be hungry after being out all night,' said Betty. 'Bruiser said you had a murder on your paws at Catberry Manor. Trouble with them posh folk is they don't know how to behave themselves, but I dare say you'll get to the bottom of it. Anyway, I'll leave you to your late lunch. We're having roast chicken for dinner if you'd like to join us? We invited Bruiser but he's having dinner with Dolly and Molly so it'll just be the four of us.'

'That sounds lovely,' said Tilly, taking the tray from Betty. 'I'm sure we can come but I'll check with Hettie and let you know. I think we have to go to the undertakers but we shouldn't be late back.'

'My word,' said Betty, 'don't you both live the high life! Murders, undertakers and all those crime fiction books you read – nothing like looking on the bright side of things. Just turn up at seven if you're free.'

Betty retreated back upstairs to her flat to join her sister, who was listening to *Gardeners' Question Time* on the radio, hoping for a few tips on getting rid of slugs and snails. Tilly went about the tricky business of waking Hettie, which proved to be much easier once she'd dangled a ham bap in front of her face.

'Is it still Sunday?' asked Hettie, yawning and stretching her paws out above her head.

'Yes,' said Tilly, preparing two mugs of milky tea, 'and the Butters have invited us for Sunday dinner later. I told Betty we'd like to come but I know we have to go and see Morbid first.'

'For two pins I'd leave all that until tomorrow,' said Hettie, talking through a mouthful of ham bap, 'but I suppose we should see what Morbid has to say about Morgana's death before we go back to the Catberrys in the morning. I'll give her a ring and see if she's about. We could have a stroll down to the undertakers and be back in time for Sunday dinner with Betty and Beryl and an early night. We'll need to be on our toes if we're facing Praline Catberry tomorrow.'

The two cats enjoyed their lunch and Hettie was in luck when she phoned Morbid. She was on duty and happy for them to call in to discuss Morgana's body.

It was a pleasant walk down the high street in the sunshine. The puddles had almost disappeared and the cats who were out and about had left their umbrellas at home and had ventured out without coats. 'It's the nicest time of the year,' said Tilly, with a spring in her step. 'Everything is so fresh and new, just like Mole when he met up with Rat by the riverbank.'

'You love that book, don't you?' said Hettie. 'I know what you mean, though. The winters seem to get longer these days so when things finally start to improve they lift your spirits in hopes of a warm summer.' Hettie slowed her pace as they reached the church. 'I just want to take a quick look in St Kipper's graveyard before we head for Sheba Gardens.'

Tilly followed Hettie into the churchyard and both cats made their way round to the side of the church where the most recent burials had taken place. It was a matter of minutes before Hettie found what she was looking for. 'Here he is,' she said, approaching a simple wooden cross bearing the name of Horace Catberry, 'and only one bunch of flowers.'

Tilly turned the flowers over to reveal a card. 'It says "Miss You. Mx". I wonder if the M stands for Morgana?'

'I wouldn't be at all surprised,' said Hettie.

'I did expect more flowers,' said Tilly. 'It looks more like one of those pauper's graves where no one cares.'

'You could be spot on there,' said Hettie. 'Come on – let's go and see what Morbid has to tell us.'

The better-heeled cats of Sheba Gardens were all busy at the front of their properties, tidying up after the ravages of winter, as Hettie and Tilly headed for Shroud and Trestle. When they reached the undertakers, even Ethel Trestle had emerged from her reception desk into the sunshine to put new compost in her pots before planting out her overwintered geraniums. She actually managed a proper smile as Hettie and Tilly approached. 'Morbid said to go in through the back door,' she said, waving her trowel in that direction.

Mr Trestle nodded to them as they made their way round to the door. He seemed pleased to have the sunshine on his back as he polished the bonnet of one of the hearses. Once inside, Hettie and Tilly knocked on the door of Morbid's preparation room. 'Come in,' she said. 'There's cake and I'm just about to put the kettle on.'

Hettie and Tilly didn't need asking twice. They pushed open the door to be confronted by a large chocolate cake balanced on the end of one of Morbid's mortuary benches, next to a variety of unmentionable items in glass jars of formaldehyde.

'It arrived this morning from a grateful customer,' said Morbid, pointing a teaspoon at the cake before stirring sugar into three mugs. 'You're going to have to help me eat it as it has fresh cream which won't last.' She approached the cake with a scalpel she'd retrieved from a sterilising unit and cut three perfect slices, placing them on some kitchen roll and laying them out on one of the wall benches. 'Perch yourselves on a couple of stools. The tea's coming up.'

Hettie and Tilly did as they were told, slightly concerned at the prospect of having tea and cake sur-rounded by the rather macabre specimens of Morbid's everyday working life, especially as the centre of the room was dominated by a body covered in a white sheet on the main mortuary table.

'Is that Morgana Catberry?' asked Tilly in hushed tones in case she disturbed the corpse.

'It certainly is,' said Morbid, passing round the mugs of tea. 'Let's eat some cake first, then I'll give you a full report.'

It didn't take Tilly long to be covered in cream and chocolate cake, which served as a welcome distraction from the surroundings, but after a cursory wipe with a cloth in Morbid's sink, she and Hettie were ready to receive Morbid's thoughts on Morgana. Tilly hung back to observe from a safe distance as Hettie moved forward towards the corpse.

'It took me a couple of hours to get that polythene stuff off her,' said Morbid, removing the sheet from Morgana's body. 'She looks like she was in some sort of fight but that's not what killed her.'

'She had a really vicious catfight with her sister-in-law on Friday night,' said Hettie.

'Ah well, that explains it – those wounds aren't fresh. But if you look here at the back of her head, she's been dragged along the ground – the fur's missing and there are bits of tarmac embedded in her skin. A combination of things contributed to her death. She's taken a couple of heavy blows to the side of her head, which may have knocked her out, but my guess is asphyxiation due to this polythene film from that shrink-wrapper machine. She obviously breathed it in while she was fighting for breath as I retrieved some of it as far back as her throat. She seems to have been very aware of what was happening to her.' Morbid pointed to a tub under the mortuary table which was full to the top with strands of polythene. 'The trouble with this stuff is it binds itself to anything with heat, so she was cooked as well as suffocated, and she had no chance of escape as her paws and legs were tied up so tightly that the skin was broken and cut into.'

'This is terrible,' said Hettie. 'It looks like we're searching for a monster.'

'And that's not the worst of it,' said Morbid. 'She was expecting kittens, with – at a guess – about three weeks to go. Sadly the kittens are all dead and I haven't attempted to remove them.'

'This whole thing just gets more horrific by the minute,' said Hettie, 'and it gives most of the Catberry family an even stronger motive for doing away with her. The last thing any of them would want is more legitimate heirs to the Catberry fortune.'

'Poor Pettifur,' said Tilly. 'Not only has he lost Morgana but his kittens as well. How will he ever recover from all of this?'

'He made no mention of Morgana expecting kittens,' Hettie pointed out, 'so maybe he didn't know, which begs the question why not?'

That particular question hung in the air for a moment before Morbid pulled the sheet back over Morgana's body and returned to the chocolate cake to cut another three slices. 'Come on, you two – it's all got to go.'

The three cats did their best to enjoy the cake but Hettie's mind was racing. She'd fully expected to be told that Morgana had died a terrible death but the added complication of kittens required a complete rethink about motive and the potential murderer. 'There don't seem to be any other Catberrys buried at St Kipper's,' she said, rinsing the cream off her paws in the sink.

'That's probably because they've got their own burial ground out at Sunny Tails,' suggested Morbid. 'Old Lockjaw Jarvis runs an undertakers of sorts in

Catberry-on-the-Brink. He's a furniture maker by trade but he knocks up a passable coffin as and when required. Nowhere near as grand as Ethel's brochure but I think he's buried most of the Catberrys over the years.'

'So why did the family have Horace Catberry buried at St Kipper's?' asked Tilly.

'I've no idea,' said Morbid. 'It was all such a rushed job, with Praline pushing to get it over with as quickly as possible. No job satisfaction in that funeral.'

'I know it's an odd sort of question but how does an exhumation work?' asked Hettie.

'Not an easy one, that,' said Morbid. 'For a start, there must be a very good reason for digging a body up and it would require the next of kin's permission unless foul play was strongly suspected. Before you even consider it, I doubt that Praline Catberry would give her consent if you were thinking about disturbing Horace from his slumbers.'

'What if we didn't ask her?' suggested Hettie. 'The grave looks fairly fresh and it wouldn't take much to shift some soil and have a quick look in his coffin.'

Tilly looked alarmed. 'Why would you want to do that?'

'Because I'd like to know what all those papers were that Praline buried with him. I honestly think that all roads lead back to the death of Horace Catberry or maybe even Caramela Catberry, Pettifur's first wife.'

Morbid looked at the calendar on the wall and traced a date with her claw. 'Well Horace has only been in the ground for three weeks, according to this, so it wouldn't be too difficult to lift him – but I'd be putting my job on the line unless I could convince Mr Shroud and Mr Trestle that there was a very good reason for doing it.'

'We've been summoned by Praline to Catberry Manor tomorrow morning so I might ask her outright what she put in Horace's coffin. In fact, I've a lot of questions to put to her, but if we fail and get chucked out I think Horace may have to see the light of day one more time.'

Morbid laughed and shook her head. 'No chance of that. Exhumations have to be done at first light, out of decency. I doubt that Horace will ever see the sun on his face again. I'd better research the process in case you want to go through with it and I'll broach the subject with my bosses if I can find the right moment. I could probably get away with opening the coffin but bringing the body back here could be a problem.'

'To be honest,' said Hettie, 'I'd settle for grabbing the papers out of the coffin. I'm not really interested in Horace.'

'What would you like me to do about Morgana? Shall I stick her in the freezer with the ginger cat for now?'

'Yes, I think that would be best,' said Hettie. 'I'll try and speak to Pettifur when we go to the Manor tomorrow. If he doesn't know already, I'll have to tell him about the kittens. Morgana's murder has rather sidetracked us from the bodies in the vat and no one so far says they recognise the ginger cat. Maybe a new week will bring a breakthrough on all counts.'

'Well, good luck with Praline Catberry,' said Morbid, seeing Hettie and Tilly out to the yard. 'I think you'll need it – and let me know about Horace if you decide to go ahead with it.'

'Thank you for the tea and cake,' said Tilly, feeling ever so slightly sick and pleased to be out in the fresh air.

Chapter Twenty-Two

It turned much colder on their walk back to the bakery as the sun went down. By the time Hettie and Tilly arrived back in their room, they were both looking forward to a hot meal, and the irresistible smell of roast chicken filled their nostrils. Tilly had managed to walk off the sickness from the chocolate cake and was now looking forward to something 'savoury', as she put it. Hettie, though keen on the prospect of a roast dinner, was greatly troubled by what she'd learnt about Morgana's death. The killing was bad enough but it needed a lot more work to make sense of who had taken her life and why she'd been so cruelly murdered.

'I think I'll have to change my cardigan,' said Tilly. 'I've got cream from Morbid's cake up one of the sleeves and the whole thing smells of undertakers. I don't know how Morbid works there every day. It's all so sad.'

'I suppose someone's got to do it,' said Hettie, pulling an almost clean T-shirt out of the filing cabinet and changing into it. 'This Lockjaw Jarvis cat sounds interesting out at Catberry-on-the-Brink. Morbid gave the impression that she didn't entirely agree with his methods. If we have time tomorrow we should take a look at that village, especially Sunny Tails as we've heard so much about it.'

'I'm not looking forward to seeing Praline tomorrow,' said Tilly, pulling on her second-best Sunday cardigan. 'In fact, I think all those Catberrys are horrid cats who deserve each other – except for Grace and Dandy.'

'What about Pettifur?' asked Hettie. 'You said you felt sorry for him.'

'I do,' said Tilly, moving towards the door, 'but I'm not sure I like him.'

The two cats climbed the stairs to the Butters' flat and received a royal welcome. Betty and Beryl regarded Hettie and Tilly as family and were always pleased to share a meal with them, especially when they were working on an interesting case.

'Come in, you two,' said Beryl. 'Sister is just getting the roasties out of the oven and I've carved the chicken. Get yourselves up the table and we'll be with you in a tick.'

The Butter sisters' flat was very comfortable and homely and had proved to be a sanctuary on several occasions for Hettie and Tilly when their murder cases had overpowered them. Although Betty and Beryl were both extroverts and keen on gossip, Hettie knew that she could trust them to be discreet when it mattered and they had even stepped forward on occasions to help solve some of the crimes by injecting some Lancashire-grown common sense.

'Knives and forks at the ready 'cause here it comes,' said Betty, putting two laden plates in front of Hettie and Tilly. 'Extra gravy in that jug if you need it.'

Beryl followed behind her sister with their dinners and the four cats put away the cares of the day to enjoy a proper Sunday roast with all the trimmings. 'So how are things going with the Catberrys?' asked Betty, leaning back in her chair and pushing her empty plate away from her. 'We were getting worried, what with you all being out all night.'

Hettie poked the last of her pigs-in-blankets into her mouth before giving a potted version of Morgana's murder and Morbid's findings. Both sisters were shocked and listened to every detail before offering their thoughts. 'Well, I call that a tragedy,' said Beryl. 'What a terrible way to go! And those poor little kittens – what sort of cat does that?'

'Trouble is, Morgana Cutlet put herself in the line of fire,' said Betty. 'She should have settled for a nice hard-working cat rather than reaching for the stars, but no one deserves to die like that. I think she was a nice cat under all that lipstick and nail varnish. Our friend Florrie Bundee lives in Sunny Tails and when we visited her just after Christmas she mentioned that Morgana was the life and soul of the place, organising lots of things for them to do.'

'Florrie said Morgana had organised a drama work-shop where they all had to pretend to be sheep,' added Beryl. 'She said she'd never laughed so much in all her days. Morgana called it method acting or something like that.'

'Is Florrie still at Sunny Tails?' asked Hettie.

'As far as we know,' said Betty. 'She used to work on the biscuits out there until she retired. She's got a lovely room overlooking the gardens.'

'We might like to visit her. Do you think she'd mind?'

'Not in the slightest,' said Beryl. 'She's a real chatterbox and loves a bit of company. You just tell her we sent you.'

'So how far are you along with Morgana's murder?' asked Betty, as she collected up the empty plates.

'It's at that stage where it could be anyone,' said Hettie. 'Nearly all the Catberrys had issues with her, and it's strange but there seem to have been two very different sides to Morgana depending on who you talk to. That's making things even more difficult.'

'Well, as our old mother used to say, it's the right parcel delivered to the wrong address,' said Beryl. 'By the sound of it, not even Morgana knew who she was and it must be hard living in a family like the Catberrys. Anyway, we have apple crumble or a baked custard tart with cling peaches – and you can have cream or ice cream.'

'What's a cling peach?' asked Tilly.

'Bless you,' said Beryl. 'It's just what it says – the peach clings to its stone, so you have to slice it away, as opposed to a free stone that comes away nicely – or you could have a semi-cling, of course.'

'Then I think I'd like the custard tart with the clings,' said Tilly.

'I'd like the apple crumble and cream,' said Hettie, even though she was full to bursting.

'Get yourselves sat down in the comfy chairs and I'll put the TV on,' said Betty, looking at her watch. 'We're just in time for the *London Palladium*. Maggot Fonteyn and Rudolph Nearenough are doing a dance tonight and Carole Kink has flown in from America according to the *Radio Times*, although we only really watch it for the beat the clock bit. Sister and me think it's fixed – you surely can't get contestants out of the audience every week who are that stupid.'

Hettie was hoping for an early escape to catch up on her sleep but the Butters seemed to be settling in for an evening of TV and congenial company. The four cats sat eating their puddings as the band struck up at the Palladium. Within minutes of finishing her pudding, Hettie was fast asleep. Tilly had a small incident with one of her cling peaches that escaped her bowl and shot into Beryl's lap, but it was recovered quickly, just as Maggot and Rudolph took their final bow.

Hettie woke up as the credits rolled across the screen and was grateful when Betty suggested that they should all think about going to bed. 'We've got a big order of pies to get to Malkin and Sprinkle first thing tomorrow,' she said, 'and you two have to get on and solve that murder so we'd better call it a night. We'll stick some pies in your room for your suppers tomorrow. We're doing lamb and shallot as it's Monday.'

'That will be lovely,' said Tilly, 'and thank you for our roast dinner.'

'You are always welcome,' said Betty, as the two sisters waved them off.

Back in their room, Hettie and Tilly settled down to sleep. They were very full and very exhausted but the prospect of an audience with Praline Catberry kept them both awake until the early hours.

Chapter Twenty-Three

Monday mornings had always been a challenge to Hettie Bagshot. It was perhaps the fear of staring down the barrel of a brand-new week, wondering what it might bring. Being a pessimist didn't help, as she rarely considered that the days ahead might bring good things rather than disasters. Tilly, by direct contrast, welcomed every day with great expectations, especially since finding a home that was safe and secure with Hettie. Their partnership had saved her from a homeless existence on the streets and being part of the Detective Agency had given her purpose and a real sense of pride. But today she lay in her fleecy blanket, dreading their meeting with Praline Catberry. She had watched the way the matriarch swept away and humiliated her own family and their concerns and wondered whether she and Hettie would be treated in the same way.

Reluctantly, she padded across to the kettle and filled it at the sink. Switching it on she prepared their tea mugs and put two slices of bread in the toaster.

She peeled the foil off two cheese triangles and made the tea. It was a ritual she normally loved but today all she really wanted to do was go back to bed.

Hettie stirred as the toast popped up and squinted at the clock on the mantelpiece. It was half past eight, and as she gradually re-entered the land of the living, leaving her dreams unfinished, she too suddenly remembered the blot on their landscape. 'It's enough to make a witch spit!' she announced, more to herself than to Tilly. 'I shall be really pleased to get this morning over with.'

'Me too,' said Tilly, spreading the cheese on the toast. 'Maybe I could sit in the sidecar and wait for you?'

'You are joking of course,' said Hettie, hauling herself into a sitting position to receive her breakfast. 'Don't think you can escape that easily. I need you to take notes and look intimidating.'

Tilly giggled at the thought and passed Hettie her tea and toast before settling on her fleecy blanket to eat her own. She was interrupted briefly by a knock at the door. Bruiser stood on the threshold with a tray of pies in his paws. 'I'm just runnin' these pies ta Malkin an' Sprinkle for Betty an' Beryl an' I'll be ready to take you to Catberry Manor at 'alf past nine if that's OK? I didn't want you ta think I'd forgotten.'

'That's lovely,' said Tilly. 'We'll see you in the high street.' She returned to her breakfast, then took on the task of finding something to wear. Her cardigans had taken a battering over the winter and regardless of continued sponging down some of the food stains refused to budge without a proper wash. 'I'm going to have to sort our washing out now it's stopped raining,' she said to one of her very best cardigans, which currently held memories of a rather overactive fried egg.

'I'm sure the Butters will let you borrow their twin-tub,' said Hettie, joining Tilly at the filing cabinet, 'but not today, even if it is Monday. Today is the day for Praline Catberry to wash her dirty laundry.'

Tilly giggled again, then chose one of the cardigans least affected by her excesses and pulled it on. Hettie chose a long-sleeved T-shirt and some rather crumpled business slacks. After two more mugs of tea and another round of cheese triangles on toast, the two cats were ready to face the day. Tilly grabbed her satchel and checked that her notepad was still in it, along with the photo of the ginger cat and the personal effects that Morbid had found in the chocolate vat.

They made their way into the high street just as Bruiser pulled up on Miss Scarlet. Tilly was first into the sidecar and Hettie was about to follow when Betty came bustling out of the bakery with a large paper bag. 'Some reinforcements for the three of you,' she said, pushing the bag at Hettie. 'We've done you a sandwich lunch with cake to keep you going and there's a Battenberg in there to sweeten your meeting with Praline.'

Hettie passed the bag to Tilly and jumped in beside her, deciding to keep the lid open as the sun was shining. Bruiser kicked the bike into life and the three cats sped off down the high street en route to Catberry-on-the-Brink. They arrived at the Manor with five minutes to spare so Hettie and Tilly decided to sit and compose themselves until Sparks appeared at the door and beckoned them across. Tilly slid the Battenberg out of their lunch bag, hoping it might act as an ice-breaker, and left Bruiser in charge of the rest.

'We shouldn't be too long,' said Hettie. 'I'd quite like to take a look round the village later.'

'Right'o,' said Bruiser, transferring himself to the sidecar with yesterday's *Sunday Snout* crossword. 'Give me a shout if you need me.'

Hettie and Tilly followed Sparks into the Manor and up the grand staircase to uncharted territory. 'The Mistress will see you in her sitting room,' he said, stopping outside one of the many doors that led off the landing. He knocked and Praline responded, instantly barking out a 'come in' and setting a strict and unwelcoming tone. Sparks opened the door and nodded for Hettie and Tilly to enter before shutting the door behind them and going about his business.

Praline moved towards them as Tilly proffered the Battenberg. 'The Butters have sent this for you with their compliments,' she said, which seemed momentarily to derail Praline's rather aggressive approach. She took the cake and abandoned it on a table, then turned back to face Hettie and Tilly. 'I'll keep this short and to the point,' she began. 'I'm not used to having strangers poking their noses into my family's affairs and it was completely without my consent that Pettifur engaged you. I have no wish for you to continue to investigate further regarding the bodies in the chocolate vat – or, for that matter, the death of Morgana. She was a silly cat who squandered all the opportunities the family was able to offer her and caused nothing but trouble from the day she arrived. I do, however, appreciate that you have spent some time doing whatever it is you do here at the Manor so I'm willing to offer you a substantial sum of money to leave my family in peace.'

Praline crossed to an ornate and very expensive looking desk by the window and picked up a cheque that she had clearly written earlier. She passed it to Hettie and pulled the bell pull by the fireplace. Sparks appeared immediately, as if he'd been on guard outside the door. 'Please show our visitors out,' she said, and without looking back left the sitting room by another door, closing it behind her.

Hettie and Tilly were completely bewildered as they followed Sparks to the front door. They had both known that the meeting with Praline was going to be difficult, but they had never expected to be given their marching orders. The business had been so swiftly concluded that Hettie hadn't even looked at the cheque.

Bruiser had barely got started on his crossword and leapt out of the sidecar, thinking there had been more trouble. Hettie, still feeling slightly shell-shocked, explained briefly that their services were no longer required before climbing into the sidecar with Tilly.

'Where now?' asked Bruiser. 'They do a nice all-day breakfast at the Brink in the village. Me an' Dolly stopped there once.'

'An excellent idea,' said Hettie, regaining her composure. 'We need to have a think and an all-day breakfast might help.'

Bruiser started up the bike and headed down the drive towards the main road to the village. They passed the entrance to the factory and continued onto a main street lined with small, terraced houses, all with neat front gardens and all painted in brown and yellow, the colours of the Catberry brand. 'These must be the workers' houses from the factory,' said Tilly. 'It's a nice idea but they all look the same. Look by the village pond – that big house must be Sunny Tails, the retirement home.'

Hettie didn't reply as she was distracted by the cheque still in her paws. She stared down at the figures, thinking they might change if she looked closer. Tilly, realising that her friend had gone very quiet, looked across at the cheque and gasped. 'Does that really say what I think it says?'

Hettie nodded as Bruiser swung the motorbike into the pub car park. 'Yes, it says five hundred pounds. All I can say is that's one very big cover-up payment.'

'What do you mean?' asked Tilly, taking the cheque and putting it safely in her satchel.

'I mean that Praline Catberry clearly has a very good idea about who murdered Morgana and probably knows about the bodies in the vat as well. That cheque is silence money and I'm damned if I'm giving up this case just because she thinks she can buy us off. Morgana deserves justice and so do the cats who ended up in The Tabby in Black chocolate.'

Hettie jumped out of the sidecar, followed by Tilly. Bruiser closed the lid in case it rained and the three cats adjourned to the bar of the Brink, where Hettie ordered three full English breakfasts.

The pub was quiet and Hettie found a table tucked away from the bar where they could discuss their situation in relative peace. The breakfasts, when they came, didn't disappoint and all three cats tucked in as if they hadn't eaten for a week. 'That was really good,' said Hettie, pushing her empty plate away from her. 'It's surprising how much of an appetite you can build up by being sacked.'

'Praline said she never wanted us to investigate,' said Tilly. 'It was Pettifur who called us so maybe he might still want us to find out who killed Morgana.'

'You could be right,' said Hettie, 'but I don't see how we can get in touch with him without Praline knowing about it if he's still living at the Manor. If he really wants us to carry on with the case, he'll get in touch – he knows where we are – but I don't see why we can't investigate on our own. We've got lots of interviews, although they could all be lying, and I'm keen to visit Sunny Tails to have a chat with Florrie Bundee. I don't know why but I think we may find some answers there, and I want to have a look at the Catberry burial ground.'

'Are you going to ask Morbid to dig up Horace Catberry?' asked Tilly, mopping up the last of her egg with a piece of toast.

'I think it might come to that but we should talk to Florrie first and then go through your notes.'

'Is there anythin' you'd like me ta do?' offered Bruiser.

'Actually yes,' said Hettie. 'While Tilly and I go and visit Florrie, you could see if you can find a character called Lockjaw Jarvis. Morbid says he lives in the village and is a sort of undertaker. It would be good to know what kind of operation he runs and what connection he has with the Catberrys and their workers.'

'OK,' said Bruiser. 'I'll 'ave a walk through the village an' see what I can turn up. I'll park Miss Scarlet at Sunny Tails first. I think she'll be safer there than leavin' 'er in the pub car park.'

'Right,' said Hettie, standing up and looking purposeful. 'Let's all meet at the village pond in about an hour for our Butters' packed lunch. Tilly and I will walk to Sunny Tails as it's such a nice day.'

Bruiser headed to the car park to collect Miss Scarlet. Hettie settled up for their breakfasts and then set out with Tilly for Sunny Tails.

The Catberrys retirement home was impressive. Built in the same style as the Manor, it sat in an idyllic plot of land turned over to formal gardens, with a substantial area for growing fruit and vegetables. The main door was wide open as Hettie and Tilly approached along a path supported on either side by a legion of daffodils and primroses. Stepping over the threshold, they were greeted by a cat chewing on a clay pipe, brandishing a basket full of leeks. 'I'm 'opin' to win this year,' he said. 'These beauties should impress them judges. I got second prize for my shallots last year but the slugs 'ave done fer me winter pansies, what with all that rain we've 'ad. Are you lookin' fer anyone in particular?'

'We've come to see Florrie Bundee,' said Hettie.

'Biscuit Florrie, you'll be wantin', he said, putting his basket of leeks down on the floor while he pulled his fob watch out of his waistcoat pocket to check the time. 'Just gone 'arf past eleven so she'll be back in 'er room after bowls practice. You might just catch 'er before she goes to Hair Rowbicks.'

'Could you point us in the direction of her room?'

'I'll do better than that,' he said, picking up his leeks. 'Follow me.'

The gardener strode off down a corridor which opened out into a sunny room full of elderly cats painting and making clay pots. 'This 'ere is the arts class for them what fancies themselves as cultured. Give me a trowel an' a nice bit of compost any day. I likes ta feel the soil under me claws – nothin' like it.' The cat moved on through the art class into another corridor and stopped at the first door. 'There yer go – safely delivered but don't play cards with 'er. She'll clean you out.'

The gardener went on his way, leaving Hettie and Tilly at Florrie's door. Hettie knocked and waited, then knocked again. This time the door was opened by a small, bright-eyed cat wearing a leotard, a head-band and bright pink legwarmers. 'I'm sorry to disturb you,' said Hettie, 'but Betty and Beryl Butter sent us and I wondered if you had time for a brief chat?'

'Well, if Betty and Beryl sent you, then you must come in,' said Florrie. 'I was about to have me elevenses out on me patio before I went off to me Hair Rowbicks.'

Hettie and Tilly followed Florrie into her room and out through some French windows onto a patio bathed in sunshine, with several chairs gathered around a pretty mosaic-tiled table. 'How do you know Betty and Beryl?' asked Florrie.

'I suppose you could say that we're their lodgers,' said Hettie.

'Fancy that!' said Florrie. 'You must be Hettie and Tilly, the detectives. Betty and Beryl were singing your praises when they visited me just after Christmas. Have a seat and I'll get you both a coffee and then you can tell me what this is all about.'

Florrie disappeared back into her room and Hettie and Tilly sat down on the chairs she'd offered to them.

'This is quite some place,' said Hettie, looking around her, 'and it seems to be really well planned. It looks like all the rooms on this side have patios which open out on to those amazing gardens.'

'And the art class looked lovely,' said Tilly. 'I've always wanted to make something out of clay.'

'Not your best idea,' said Hettie, 'not with your reputation for mess. If you can't keep a cling peach under control, what hope is there for a potter's wheel?'

Tilly giggled as Florrie joined them with a tray of coffees and a tin of biscuits bearing the unmistakable Catberry logo. 'There you go,' she said, passing out the coffees. 'Made with hot milk, just like it should be. Help yourself to biscuits – all homegrown, of course.'

'I gather you worked for the Catberrys in their biscuit department?' said Hettie, avoiding the Mog Nobs and selecting a chocolate claw from the tin that Florrie proffered.

'Yes, that's right. I started in packing as a kitten and rose through the ranks to digestives and misshapes, although I did do a spell in chocolate claws just before Miss Rhubarb took over. She promoted me to digestives and I was very happy there.'

'What was Miss Rhubarb like as a boss?' asked Hettie, dipping her chocolate claw into her coffee.

'I think the modern word is driven,' said Florrie, offering the tin to Tilly, who bravely chose a Mog Nob. 'She's a cat who likes things to be perfect and expects everyone around her to knuckle down and do as she says. I hope you don't think I'm speaking out of turn, but to be honest none of the current Catberrys are particularly nice cats. Mr Horace was lovely and Miss Morgana really supports us all here, even though Miss Praline would like to see Sunny Tails closed down. Mind you, Miss Morgana isn't really one of them, is she?'

Hettie swallowed hard at the realisation that news doesn't always travel fast. 'I'm afraid there's some really bad news about Morgana,' she said. 'She died on Saturday night and it was no accident. We're investigating her murder.'

Florrie froze for a moment or two, staring into her coffee as she clutched the mug tightly in both paws. Eventually she lifted her head and Hettie could see that there were tears in her eyes. 'It was never going to end well,' Florrie said. 'The trouble with this life is you have to cherish the happy times, as there's always something nasty and unexpected waiting in the wings.'

'In what way?' asked Hettie, as Tilly pulled her notepad out of her satchel.

'Well, it's no secret here at Sunny Tails that Mr Horace had a real fancy for Morgana and she for him. They spent a lot of time together here and they were very happy times for us all. Miss Morgana worked really hard to make this place a success, with lovely trips out, but all that stopped when Mr Horace died and we've hardly seen Morgana since then. We've all been a bit worried lately about what might happen next but I understood from Morgana that Mr Horace was going to leave the place to her in his will. I don't know if that ever happened. What will happen now?'

'My understanding is that Lolly Catberry thinks she stands to inherit,' said Hettie, hoping for a reaction. She wasn't disappointed.

'Miss Lolly, you say!' spat out Florrie. 'She's a nasty piece of work at the best of times. Miss Praline sent her here just before Christmas, supposedly to have a rest, but really she spent the whole time snooping on Morgana and Mr Horace. That was just after Praline's sister died.'

'I didn't know she had a sister,' said Hettie. 'Did she work for the Catberrys?'

'I suppose you could say indirectly,' said Florrie. 'She was the poor relative. Praline took pity on her and gave her a job here in the kitchens. Nice enough cat, but nervous and always grateful, if you know what I mean. I must say she used to get on my nerves but it was sad when she died. Cut herself chopping onions and it went septic, poor thing. Gone in a week she was.'

'Was Miss Praline close to her sister?'

'Not really,' said Florrie. 'As far as I know, she never visited her here and didn't come to the funeral. In fact, I can't remember a time when Miss Praline came here at all, not even after Ginger died. It was left to Mr Horace to make the arrangements.'

Hettie shared a look with Tilly, daring to hope that they were finally getting somewhere with the identification of one of the bodies in the chocolate. 'Was that with Lockjaw Jarvis?' Hettie suggested.

'That's right. Miserable old cat – no one here likes to see him coming up the drive with his tape measure.'

'You mentioned that Praline's sister was called Ginger – was that her real name?'

Florrie shook her head. 'No. According to the plaque in the burial ground, her name was Verity Tinker. Ginger was a nickname, as far as I know.'

'So is she buried there?' asked Hettie.

'In a manner of speaking,' said Florrie. 'Her ashes are. Lockjaw Jarvis cremates all the Sunny Tails residents except for the Catberrys – they have their own mausoleum just beyond the allotment. It's quite some place too – built by Hauxston Catberry back in Victorian times. Lovely gardens all round it. You should have a walk up there.'

Hettie's heart began to beat faster as she signalled to Tilly, who instantly pulled the photo of the ginger cat out of her satchel. 'I have a photograph of a cat who sadly has died and I wonder if you'd be kind enough to see if you recognise her? I'm afraid you may find the picture upsetting.'

Undaunted by Hettie's warning, Florrie took the photograph and reached for the magnifying glass on the patio table. Taking a closer look, she tutted before passing the picture back to Hettie. 'That's Ginger all right. She had those lovely stripes on her head – but who on earth took a picture of her after she'd died?'

Hettie could have hugged Florrie but instead she asked Tilly for the envelope of personal effects that Morbid had found in the chocolate and turned them out on the patio table. 'Do you recognise any of these?' she asked.

Florrie picked the items up one by one until she'd looked at them all. 'Those spectacles seem familiar, but that ear stud I do recognise as I always thought how lovely it was. That belonged to Old Ned, the Catberrys' butler. He died just after I retired here, but I used to see him up at the Manor sometimes – a really handsome black cat, he was. His brother had a spell at Sunny Tails too – he was the chauffeur to the Catberrys before he retired. His name was Finch if my memory serves me well. He was a ginger. His sons work there now, of course.'

'You mean Sparks and Perks?'

'Yes, that's right. Nice boy cats – always so polite when you meet them.'

'And the spectacles – you thought they might be familiar?'

'They are,' said Florrie, 'but I can't quite place them at the moment. I'm sure it'll come back to me. I hate being old. My brain has run out of storage space, I think. I need one of those extensions like they build onto houses.'

'What do you think to Mr Pettifur?' asked Hettie, keen to keep the older cat's mind on the investigation.

Florrie chuckled before answering. 'You mean Billy Bluster,' she said. 'That's what we call him – all puffed up with importance but a shadow of his father, Mr Horace. I never understood what Miss Morgana saw in him. It's no surprise that she preferred a more mature kind of cat.'

'Some say that Morgana was a fortune hunter?' offered Hettie.

'She certainly had an eye for a comfortable lifestyle but to be honest, with looks like hers, she could have charmed any number of rich cats. It was different with Mr Horace, though. I would say they really cared for each other. You could see that when they were together. Marrying Pettifur was the worst mistake she ever made but Mr Horace encouraged it. Maybe that was so he could see more of her himself.'

'Did the rest of the family know about them?'

'Well, as I said, Miss Lolly was sent to spy on them so I'm sure Miss Praline had her suspicions. Miss Rhubarb's husband, Oliver, was sweet on Morgana too, but I don't think anything came of it, and Mr Pettifur was so wrapped up in trying to run the business that he hardly noticed anything on the domestic front. I think Mr Horace was keeping him busy so he could have more time with Morgana but I can't believe that she's dead.'

'I gather you like a game of cards?' said Hettie. 'If you had to place a bet, who would you say would be most likely to have murdered Morgana?'

'I'd definitely hope for a royal flush in my paw! With the exception of Pettifur's young daughters, any one of that family is capable of murder. The sooner Grace and Dandy inherit the business, the better off we'll all be – if we're still here.'

'You've been very helpful,' said Hettie, getting to her feet as Tilly collected up the photograph and the personal effects from the patio table and pushed them into her satchel. 'I hope we haven't held you up from your activities for too long.'

'It's been a pleasure to have some company from outside this place,' said Florrie. 'I hope I haven't let my tongue run away with me too much. You're very easy to talk to. I can see why Betty and Beryl have such a high opinion of you both. Send them my best wishes and tell them not to leave it too long before they come and see me. At my age you can never plan ahead too far but I hope you catch the cat who murdered poor Morgana. I'll have to be the bearer of that sad news at lunch today. A lot of us will really miss her.'

Florrie waved her visitors off and Hettie and Tilly left by her patio and made their way through the gardens to the front of the building, where Bruiser was waiting for them by Miss Scarlet. 'Time for lunch, I think,' suggested Hettie. 'We've certainly got plenty of food for thought, as well as the Butters' packed picnic.'

Bruiser leaned into the sidecar to retrieve the paper bag and the three cats made their way to a bench by the village pond. Tilly, who loved listing things, decided to give them a rundown of the contents of the paper bag and Hettie and Bruiser listened with

interest. 'We've got three doorstep chicken sandwiches, so that's one each; three packets of cheese and
onion crisps; three cooked sausages; and three large
slices of Victoria sandwich.'

Deciding to leave their discussions until after lunch,
Hettie and Bruiser made a start on their sandwiches
and Tilly – true to form – started with the cake and
worked backwards, finishing with her sandwich. It had
been a warm sunny morning but, as they poked the
final pieces of their lunch into their mouths, several
black clouds appeared to obscure the sun. Suddenly it
became much colder.

'Let's call in at the Brink for a milky tea,' suggested
Hettie. 'I don't like the look of that sky and I'm dying
to find out how you got on with Lockjaw Jarvis.'

Tilly and Bruiser laughed at Hettie's unintentional
joke regarding the village undertaker as they headed
back to Miss Scarlet. Bruiser drove them the short distance to the pub, where the landlord welcomed them
back as his only customers now that the lunchtime
rush was over.

Chapter Twenty-Four

'So come on, tell us about Lockjaw Jarvis,' said Hettie, stirring two sugar lumps into her milky tea.

'It took me a while ta find 'im as it's just an ordinary 'ouse, but 'e's really creepy – keeps twistin' 'is paws an' stickin' 'is 'ead on one side. I pretended that I was makin' arrangements for an old aunt tha's just died an' 'e offered me several possibilities. 'E said 'e could do me a cheap deal as long as I didn't want 'er body back, as 'e 'ad 'is own cremator an' sold the ashes on as compost. 'E took me out into 'is back yard an' showed me this big old oven an' I couldn't quite believe what I was seein'. There were a few coffins stacked up in the yard an' 'e told me that 'e kept 'is costs down by reusin' 'em. I asked 'im what sort of customers 'e 'ad, an' 'e said 'e 'ad a good trade comin' from Sunny Tails an' looked after the Catberrys' mausoleum as well as makin' furniture. I certainly wouldn't trust 'im with the body of anyone I cared about. I'm surprised them Catberrys 'ave anything ta do with 'im.'

'I'm not,' said Hettie. 'I suspect he was the perfect undertaker for the Catberrys. No scruples, easily manipulated and keen on sharp practice.' Hettie and Tilly went on to tell Bruiser about their conversation with Florrie and how she'd identified at least two of the cats found in The Tabby in Black vat.

'The trouble is,' said Tilly, 'now that we've been sacked, I don't see what we can do about it – and we're no nearer to finding the cat who murdered Morgana.'

'I think we probably are,' said Hettie. 'I bet Sparks and Perks would be interested in knowing that their father's and uncle's bodies may have been used to enhance the flavour of Catberrys chocolate. And after what Florrie told us, there doesn't seem to be much love lost between the folk in the retirement home and the family. At first sight, it all seemed so harmonious, but now we're digging a bit deeper the worms are starting to crawl out.'

'I wonder if Praline knows that her sister was in the vat?' said Tilly.

'That's a very good question, and one I would love her to answer, but if she did know and Horace was responsible that's a very good motive for murder.'

'But why Morgana?' asked Bruiser.

'I didn't mean Morgana,' Hettie explained. 'I meant Horace. I still don't buy in to the choking on a Mog Nob story, and if Praline suspected him of disposing of her sister's body and getting too close to Morgana, the case could easily be solved. The problem is stopping her from getting away with it. From what we know, it could even be a conspiracy between Lolly, Rhubarb, Oliver and Praline.'

'What about Pettifur?' suggested Tilly. 'It might have been him that put the bodies in the vat as he worked so closely with Horace, although I can't see him killing Morgana – not like that anyway.'

'Who can say?' said Hettie. 'But you have lots of notes and I think we should go home and go through them to see if there's anything we've missed. Tomorrow I'll give Morbid a call and see if she's up for an exhumation. The deeper we get into this case, the more I'm convinced that the answers lie in Horace Catberry's coffin.'

'If she needs a pair of paws ta dig 'im up, I'm 'appy ta 'elp,' said Bruiser, 'an' I could get Poppa ta 'elp as well.'

Poppa was the town's plumber but he was also a much-used pair of extra paws in Hettie's detective agency, as and when required. Poppa and Hettie's friendship went all the way back to Hettie's music days when he had been her roadie, driving her up and down the country with her band. Like Bruiser, he was resourceful and reliable. He also walked out occasionally with Molly Bloom from the café and was considered to be very much part of Hettie and Tilly's extended family.

'That's a great idea,' said Hettie. 'I'll let Morbid know and see what she says. It's going to be a risky business digging Horace up without Praline's permission, but with you and Poppa wielding the spades, we should get it over with in no time.'

The three cats paid for their milky teas and stepped out into the Brink's car park, where puddles were forming and the rain was once again bucketing down. They made a mad dash for Miss Scarlet, but still got soaked. Bruiser gave the bike full throttle and they roared out of the pub car park, heading into the town. He dropped Hettie and Tilly off at the bakery before retiring to his shed to dry out and enjoy the pie that the Butters had left for him.

Hettie and Tilly were pleased to see that they too had had a delivery of lamb and shallot pies, although they were still both quite full from lunch. Tilly decided to make two mugs of milky tea and crawl into her pyjamas. Hettie also abandoned her own wet things and pulled her dressing gown on before lighting a fire. In a matter of minutes, their room was warm and cosy and the two cats settled down to review Tilly's notes.

'Where would you like me to start?' asked Tilly, making herself comfortable on her fleecy blanket.

'Let's look at the interviews we did after Morgana's body was found. I think the bodies in the vat are separate to that murder and we don't want to confuse things at this stage.'

'I've made a quick note about what Praline said before we started the interviews so I'll start there. She said she didn't see Morgana after Friday evening. She said she'd spent Saturday in her rooms after breakfast and was visited by Lolly, who spent some time with her. She didn't mention what she did on Saturday evening so as far as we know she hasn't got an alibi. She also didn't mention that Pettifur visited her after the row at breakfast on Saturday morning.'

'Well, she can go to the top of the suspects list, especially now she's tried to pay us off,' said Hettie.

'I think I'll start a new one just for Morgana's murder,' said Tilly, finding a clean page and scribbling 'Praline Catberry' at the top of it before turning back to her interview pages. 'We spoke to Pettifur first in the library. He told us that the last time he saw Morgana was in her room on Saturday morning, as she was too sore from the fight with Lolly to go down to breakfast. He mentioned the row at breakfast over closing the factory and that he'd gone there with Oliver to shut it all down. He said he'd called in to see Morgana at seven in the evening, but she wasn't in her room. He thought she might have walked into the village. He spent the evening doing paperwork in the library. Sparks brought him a drink at ten and Grace and Dandy dropped in to see him around one o'clock after their gig. He said the night watch cat called him after that to say the shrink-wrap machine was still on and he went to the factory and discovered Morgana's body. He called us around two-thirty. He didn't mention that he'd called in to see Praline before he left for the factory on Saturday morning, either.'

'Mmm,' said Hettie, reaching for her catnip pipe and filling it. 'I think you can safely stick him on the suspects list as he seemed to have a lot of time on his paws on Saturday night. That library has French windows. He could easily have gone out and come back without anyone noticing, but he did seem genuinely cut up about Morgana's death and I can't see a clear motive for him murdering her in such an awful way. The other thing we should consider is that he's hardly likely to murder his own kittens – if indeed they were his; we don't even know if he knew Morgana was pregnant. Too many unanswered questions there, but let's move on.'

'Lolly Catberry next,' said Tilly. 'She told us that she last saw Morgana on Friday night when they were fighting each other. She said she had breakfast in bed on Saturday morning, as she felt unwell after the fight. She visited Praline at lunchtime in her rooms and spent the afternoon with her. She went back to her room, where Sparks brought her a supper tray, and she was asleep by ten. Grace woke her in the middle of the night to tell her about Morgana. I've also made a note of the fact that she has shares in Sunny Tails, expects to inherit it all now Morgana is dead, and she will probably sell it – although Pettifur did seem to think that he might inherit Morgana's shares. And she pretended not to recognise the photo of the dead ginger cat, even though we now know it was her aunt.'

'Good point and we witnessed for ourselves that Lolly clearly hated Morgana. I suppose the possibility of inheriting Sunny Tails is a strong motive, as that place must be worth a fortune, and she could have gone out at any time on Saturday evening so she's definitely one for your list.'

Tilly added Lolly to her growing list and turned to Rhubarb Crumbwell's page. 'Rhubarb admitted straight away to us that she didn't like Morgana. She said she was nothing but trouble. She seems to have been the last cat to see Morgana as she said she saw her walking down the drive at about eight on Saturday evening. Rhubarb said she had a tray in her room around seven and then went down to the day room to watch TV – that's when she saw Morgana in the drive. She said she watched *The African Queen* on TV, as Katherine Catburn is her favourite actress. She went to bed around ten and said Oliver was already fast asleep. She was woken later by Dandy, who told her Morgana was dead. She also got upset when we showed her the dead cat photo but said she didn't recognise her.'

'There's a lot to unpick there,' said Hettie, sucking on her pipe. 'The headline is that she seemed to be the only member of the family or staff to actually see Morgana on Saturday night and if we're to believe her we must assume that Morgana was murdered after eight o'clock. But we must also ask ourselves why Morgana was out at that time? It wasn't the nicest of evenings and hardly the weather for a walk into the village.'

'Unless she was meeting someone,' said Tilly.

'Exactly. If we knew who that might be, we most likely have our killer, but it also suggests that she knew them well enough to go out and meet them on such a miserable night,' said Hettie, abandoning her pipe in the hearth and reaching for the *Radio Times*. She turned to the Saturday page. 'Well, *The African Queen* was on from eight until nine forty-five, so she got that bit right, but it's a well-known film so anyone could say they'd seen it on Saturday night. Not exactly a strong alibi.'

'And I suppose we only have her word for Morgana going down the drive at eight,' said Tilly, 'especially as no one else we've spoken to saw Morgana that afternoon or evening.'

'Precisely,' said Hettie, 'and she seemed keen to give Oliver an alibi, saying he was with Perks and then fast asleep by ten.'

'I've also made a note of her saying that Oliver should have taken over the factory and not Pettifur. She said with her in biscuits and Oliver in chocolate they'd have made a good team.'

'A spot of wishful thinking there,' said Hettie. 'She seems to have forgotten about Grace and Dandy's claim to their inheritance, although if Morgana had lived those kittens she was expecting could really have muddied the waters as far as the line of succession goes. That's a huge motive for getting rid of Morgana and the kittens all in one go. I also think that Rhubarb would be perfectly capable of murder so onto your list she goes.'

Tilly added Rhubarb and turned to Oliver Crumbwell's page. 'Oliver seemed to like Morgana and said he felt sorry for her. Florrie Bundee told us that he was sweet on her so that might be significant if we are thinking that Rhubarb might be our killer, especially if she knew about the kittens and thought they might be Oliver's.'

'Another cracking motive,' said Hettie, casting her eye across to the table where their pies sat next to two of the Butters' custard tarts. 'Let's get Oliver done and take a break for supper.'

'OK,' said Tilly. 'Oliver said that the last time he saw Morgana was on Friday night. He was at breakfast on Saturday morning when Praline announced that she was closing the factory. He said he was really angry about it and went with Pettifur to shut it all down. He left the factory at lunchtime to go to the pub in the village and he said that Pettifur went to the office to do some paperwork. Oliver met up with some of the factory workers in the pub and they had a lock-in. He told us that he went back to Perks's flat to sober up and play cards. When he left Perks, he went out for some fresh air close to the factory and suddenly remembered hearing a machine and thinking it was the refrigeration unit. Looking back, he admitted that it might have been the shrink-wrapper. He said he was in bed by ten so that puts him at the factory around nine.'

Hettie got up from her chair and collected the pies from the table, passing one to Tilly. She rested hers on the arm of her chair and added another shovelful of coal to the fire. 'The thing that gets me about this case is how isolated all these cats are – watching TV on their own, doing paperwork, wandering about in the fresh air or taking a solitary tray in their room and going to bed. No one can corroborate anyone's alibi, as they all seemed to be on their own around the time that Morgana was murdered. I'm beginning to wonder if all of them are in it together and that's why Praline paid us off. Morgana certainly rocked the boat by marrying into the family; the fact that she was expecting kittens whom everyone might assume were Pettifur's gave her the ultimate power. It all depends on Horace's will. If a boy kitten had been born to Morgana, would he have automatically succeeded Pettifur, leapfrogging over Grace and Dandy? Not only would that have dashed their hopes, but as Rhubarb and Oliver seem so keen to snatch the business away from Pettifur, a new male heir would certainly have put a fly in the ointment – even worse if the kittens turned out to be Oliver's or even Horace Catberry's. That would be the perfect motive for murder. I doubt that Pettifur knew Morgana was pregnant because I think he would have told us.'

'I just had a thought,' said Tilly. 'If Dandy and Grace spoke to Pettifur in the study at one o'clock, they would still have had time to go to the factory and murder Morgana before Pettifur discovered the body and called us, especially as it appears they could have a motive if they knew Morgana was expecting kittens.'

'That's a very good point, but if that's the case, what was Morgana doing from eight o'clock until after one? Or did she go for a walk and return to her room, then go out later to meet someone – even Dandy and Grace, as you suggest?'

Tilly nibbled the pastry crust from around her pie as she considered Hettie's thoughts. She then lifted the lid of the pie and clawed the filling out to eat before posting the rest of the pastry into her mouth, eventually wiping her paws on her fleecy blanket. Hettie disposed of her pie by taking healthy bites until it was all gone. Fortified, Tilly leapt up to make two milky teas, giving her paws a cursory wash in the sink. She delivered Hettie's custard tart to her armchair and ate her own while she was waiting for the kettle to boil. Delivering a tea to Hettie, she took hers over to her blanket and took up her notepad again.

'We've got brief statements from Sparks and his brother Perks,' said Tilly. 'Perks confirmed that Oliver was playing cards with him on Saturday evening and that he met him outside the Brink pub in the afternoon, worse for drink. He said Oliver left him to go back to the Manor just before nine o'clock. Sparks confirmed all the tray deliveries to the various family members on Saturday, but he also told us that Pettifur had seen Praline in her rooms on Saturday morning after the row at breakfast and was thinking of moving out of the Manor to a house he owned in the village, where he was going to take up gardening.'

'That sounds like a very angry cat lashing out at anyone who'll listen,' said Hettie, 'but it's interesting that he didn't mention Morgana in his future plans, especially as – according to Grace – he announced at breakfast that morning that he was resigning and going away with Morgana. Shortly after seeing Praline in her rooms, he's suddenly moving into a house in the village.'

'Maybe Praline told him something about Morgana that made him change his mind?' suggested Tilly.

'I think you might just have put your claw on it. We need to arrange another conversation with Petti-fur Catberry. Maybe Grace or Dandy could arrange for us to meet up with him away from the Manor.'

'That's a good idea,' said Tilly, 'but what are we going to do about The Tabby in Black bodies now we think we know who two of them are and the other ginger could easily be Ned's brother Finch?'

'I can't help but feel that the only crime committed there is putting them into the chocolate and I'm not sure we'll ever get to the bottom of that. It seems to me that one of the Catberrys had some sort of racket going with Lockjaw Jarvis and I'd put money on it being Horace but don't ask me why. Maybe the answer can be found in his coffin so I'll get on to Morbid in the morning. I think we'd better get some sleep – tomorrow could end up being another busy day.'

Tilly added Grace, Dandy, Oliver and Pettifur to her suspects list and settled in her blanket. Hettie pulled her dressing gown around her, sinking into her armchair. Both cats jumped as the telephone began to ring in the staff sideboard. Tilly responded by hauling the machine out onto the rug by the fire. 'The No. 2 Feline Detective Agency,' she said. 'Tilly speaking, how may I help? Oh hello Florrie – are you all right? What's that? You're at a disco and you remembered what? Yes, I understand, and thank you very much.'

Tilly replaced the receiver and pushed the telephone back into its cushions in the sideboard before facing Hettie. 'You'll never guess,' she said, 'but Florrie says the spectacles we showed her belonged to Caramela Catberry!'

Chapter Twenty-Five

It was the sunshine streaming through their small window that woke Tilly, long after the Butter sisters had fired up their bread ovens. Tilly squinted at her Top Cat alarm clock and was a little shocked to see that it was gone eleven and half the morning had disappeared. She padded to the kettle and filled it at the sink, enjoying the sun on her face as she waited for it to boil. Their small window overlooked the Butters' backyard and garden and she noticed that Bruiser was busy mowing the lawn. He'd offered himself as Betty and Beryl's lad about the yard after they had had a shed built for him and Miss Scarlet at the bottom of their garden, and he willingly paid them back by being indispensable when he wasn't working with Hettie and Tilly.

Tilly opened the cupboard over the sink and realised that they were running very low on supplies. They were down to their last few tea bags and sugar lumps; her emergency supply of custard creams had dwindled to just two; and the cheese triangles had become critical. 'I'm going to have to go down to Malkin and Sprinkle to do a proper shop,' she said, addressing the two mugs she was preparing, 'and as it's sunny I think I'll ask Betty and Beryl if I can put a wash on.'

'Good idea,' came a voice from behind her as Hettie sat up and yawned. 'That was a lovely long sleep with not a Catberry in sight. I dreamt that we were having a week at Minnie Meakin's guest house in Felixtoe, but without the murders.'

Tilly giggled as she passed Hettie her tea, remembering one of their recent high-profile cases. 'It would be lovely to have a holiday this year,' she said, 'and Minnie said we could stay there any time we wanted for free.'

'It's not like we can't afford it,' said Hettie. 'I fully intend to take the cheque that Praline Catberry gave us and wave it in front of Lavender Stamp's nose before she puts it into our savings account. She'll be so shocked she might have to shut for the day and have a lie down.'

'But if we're still investigating, maybe we shouldn't take her money,' said Tilly, sipping her tea. 'It feels like false pretences if we keep the cheque.'

'To be honest, by the time everything comes out in the wash we'll have earned every penny of that money. Morgana deserves justice, not to mention those poor cats in the chocolate who were clearly denied decent burials – and as for one of them being Pettifur's first wife Caramela, I'm wondering how Grace and Dandy might feel about that if they knew. We mustn't forget there's a vicious killer still at large and he or she might be planning to work their way through the family.'

'Speaking of things coming out in the wash,' said Tilly, 'we've got no clean clothes so I'd better get on with the washing, then go and do some shopping. We've nothing in.'

'That sounds like a plan,' said Hettie. 'I'll go and fetch us something from the bakery for breakfast and ask about the twin-tub. Stick the kettle on again and I'll be back in a minute.'

Hettie was good to her word and returned with four hot cross buns that Beryl had buttered for her. 'I thought we'd have these as a treat,' she said, clambering over the mountain of dirty clothes that Tilly had mined from the drawer of the filing cabinet in her absence. 'I told them how helpful Florrie was and they're going to visit her later this afternoon, so I think she'll be pleased to have some company. Betty said to help ourselves to the twin-tub.'

'I've put the mugs ready for the tea but I'm just going to put the first load on,' said Tilly, pulling out all the T-shirts and business slacks. 'I'll have to do my cardigans in a separate wash as Beryl says I shouldn't mix woollens with cottons.'

'It all sounds a bit technical to me,' said Hettie, before taking a healthy bite out of one of the buns, 'but I'm sure Beryl knows best. It'll just be nice to have some clean clothes.'

Tilly stumbled out of the door with the clothes she'd selected and tossed them into the twin-tub parked by the bread ovens. She took a bucket and filled it from the Butters' deep sink, then poured the water over the clothes and added a cup of soap powder from the box on the floor. She shut the lid, set the dial for cottons and pressed the on switch. The machine made a happy gurgling sound before going about its work. Tilly skipped back into their room, ready to take possession of her two hot cross buns.

'I'd better give Morbid a call,' said Hettie, posting the final piece of her bun into her mouth. 'I'm determined to find out what's in Horace's coffin, even if I have to dig him up myself, and we'd better find a way of getting in touch with Grace or Dandy. We haven't actually spoken to them about Morgana's murder and we definitely need to speak to Pettifur again without Praline knowing what we're up to. Perhaps Grace and Dandy could set that up for us.'

'Maybe we should send Grace and Dandy a telegram,' Tilly suggested. 'We could ask them to give us a call, although we run the risk of Praline intercepting it, but if Sparks gets it I'm sure he'll pass it on to them.'

'Good idea. I'll send it when I pay the cheque in at the post office,' said Hettie, draining her mug, 'but I'll call Morbid first. As you're busy with our washing, I could do the shopping if you make me a list?'

Tilly finished her hot cross bun, wiped the butter off her face with the sleeve of one of the cardigans waiting to be washed and pulled the telephone out of the staff sideboard. Hettie dialled the undertakers and Ethel put her through to Morbid. After a brief conversation, in which Hettie was at her persuasive best, the mortician agreed to the exhumation on the understanding that Bruiser and Poppa would assist with the digging and that they would all meet at St Kipper's at five the following morning.

Hettie replaced the receiver, satisfied that at last she was going to meet the cat she'd heard so much about even though he'd been dead for several weeks. 'Right,' she said, 'tin hat at the ready – I'm off to do battle with Lavender Stamp at the post office and we'd better let Bruiser know about tomorrow morning. I hope he can get hold of Poppa.'

'I'll go and find him,' said Tilly. 'I want to check on the washing anyway.'

The two cats went about their tasks. Tilly found Bruiser weeding the Butters' spring garden but Hettie's visit to Lavender Stamp proved to be a little more complicated. Lavender's queue was long and unnecessarily slow-moving; in true Lavender fashion, she fielded each of her customer's requests with a pedantic question and answer session. While Hettie waited her turn, several cats in front of her gave up and left the queue, having better things to do with their day. As she shuffled forward, Hettie considered the customer awareness course that Lavender had so recently been forced to attend and wondered what good it had done. The queue was as long as it ever was and at least three customers were reduced to tears as she waited. The mantra of the customer always being right clearly didn't exist in Lavender's world.

'Yes!' said Lavender, when Hettie's turn finally arrived.

'I'd like to send a telegram,' said Hettie, 'to Grace and Dandy Catberry at Catberry Manor in Catberry-on-the-Brink.'

Lavender stared out of her winged spectacles, then blinked before commencing battle. 'I'm well aware of where Catberry Manor is but you might have missed the post van for today so I suggest you write a letter instead.'

'But I don't want to write a letter,' said Hettie. 'I want to send a telegram. Have I missed the post van or not?'

Lavender ignored the question and took up her biro. 'What do you want to say?'

'Grace and Dandy, please contact us urgently at The No. 2 Feline Detective Agency. Regards, Hettie Bagshot.'

Lavender took her time in writing the message down before turning away to type it up on her machine and stick the words onto an official telegram form. She folded the paper, placed it in an envelope and addressed it before turning back to Hettie. 'That will be one pound and twenty pence but I can't guarantee delivery for today,' she said, looking past Hettie to the next customer.

Hettie put the money on the counter and Lavender clawed it under her grill, making much of ringing it up in the till. Much to her annoyance, when Lavender looked back expecting to see the next customer, Hettie was still there, waving Praline Catberry's cheque and her savings pass book. 'I'd like to pay this cheque into my savings account please.'

Lavender snatched the cheque out of Hettie's paw and took a closer look at it. 'This is for five hundred pounds,' she snapped. 'You're going to have to explain how you got this money before we go any further. Mrs Catberry is a favoured customer here at the post office and I find it hard to understand why she would be signing a cheque to you for this amount of money.'

'She's also a favoured customer of mine,' said Hettie, moving closer to Lavender's grill so that the cats waiting behind her couldn't hear. 'I'm sure I can trust your discretion but this cheque is hush money. You see, I know some things about the Catberrys that no one else does and Mrs Catberry knows I know and has given me this so that no one else will know. I can't tell you what I know or she might know, so would you be kind enough to add this to my savings account?'

Lavender's whiskers were twitching violently and her glasses descended onto the tip of her nose as she opened Hettie's pass book, adding the cheque to the balance and stamping the book viciously with her date stamp. 'You do know that this cheque will take three working days to clear,' she hissed, forcing the cheque onto a spike next to the till. 'I'd advise you not to rely on the money until then.'

Lavender forced the pass book back under her grill and Hettie beamed and winked at her. 'Thank you so much for your help today. It's always a pleasure to come and spend time in the post office. It really makes my day.'

Hettie grabbed her savings book and turned towards the door as the next customer received the full force of Lavender's anger, fresh from the humiliation she had suffered at Hettie's paws. In spite of what Lavender had told her, the post van drew up outside the post office as Hettie was crossing the road and she was satisfied that her telegram would be on its way to Catberry Manor before too long.

Tilly was pegging out her first line of washing when Hettie got back and the cardigans were already languishing in the twin-tub. Hettie joined her in the garden with the triumphant news that the telegram was on its way and the cheque was safely in their savings account. Bruiser, who was now planting potatoes in Beryl's vegetable patch, had managed to get hold of Poppa and had arranged with him to meet up at St Kipper's in the morning – or as Poppa had said, in 'the middle of the bloody night!'.

Hettie and Tilly spent the rest of the day on the domestic front. Tilly managed to get all her washing done and dried and Hettie sauntered down the high street to Malkin and Sprinkle, clutching the shopping list that Tilly had prepared for her. The only cat capable of reading Tilly's writing was Tilly but Hettie made the best of the list by choosing all her own favourites from the food hall as well as the essentials that they'd run out of.

By dinner time, the bottom drawer of the filing cabinet was full of neatly folded clean clothes, their cupboard was full of tasty treats and the Butters had delivered two steak pies and two cream horns for their supper before going out to visit Florrie at Sunny Tails.

They were about to sit down to their supper with one of Agatha Crispy's Miss Marble mysteries, starring Joan Hiccup, when a knock came at their door. Before Tilly had the chance to open it, both Butter sisters barged in looking distraught. 'Sorry to interrupt your supper,' said Betty, 'but we've just got back from visiting Florrie and she was in a right state. She told us that Lolly Catberry had called a meeting this lunchtime and announced that she was selling Sunny Tails so they would all have to move out by Easter.'

'And that's not the worst of it,' said Beryl, pulling a piece of paper out of her pocket and passing it to Hettie. 'This was shoved under Florrie's door this afternoon.'

Hettie looked at the note and read it out. '"If you don't want to end up as compost, you'd better keep your mouth shut." Charming,' she commented. 'I'm not surprised that Florrie is in a state and it looks like being our fault. If we hadn't visited her, this note probably wouldn't have happened.'

'And where are all those elderly cats going to go when Lolly sells up?' said Tilly.

Betty shook her head. 'That's the question they're all asking. It's shameful after all the years of service those cats have given to the Catberrys – to be turned out of homes they were promised for the rest of their lives is a scandal.'

'My immediate concern is Florrie,' said Hettie. 'We still have a murderer on the loose who won't think twice about killing an elderly cat from Sunny Tails.'

'We did suggest that she came and stayed with us,' said Beryl, 'but she insisted that she wasn't going to be driven out of her home and she wanted to stay to support the residents' campaign to keep Sunny Tails open. They've got Hacky Redtop from the *Daily Snout* going over there tomorrow to talk to them and write it up for his newspaper.'

'I can't believe that Praline Catberry would stand by and let that daughter of hers close the place down,' added Betty. 'Florrie said it was the pride and joy of Horace – and Sylvester Catberry before him. That whole village was created to look after the workers from cradle to grave.'

'I'm not sure that Praline Catberry cares much for Sunny Tails,' said Hettie, 'or the chocolate factory, for that matter. It seems that Horace Catberry wasn't exactly in her good books before he died either.'

'Ooh,' said Beryl, 'you obviously know more about it than we do.'

'Praline is actually quite nasty,' said Tilly. 'In fact, most of the Catberrys are nasty and we think one of them might have murdered Morgana. We've had to put them all on our suspects list.'

'Well we have every confidence in you both, don't we, Sister?' said Betty, 'so we'll leave you to your suppers.'

'We need to be up very early tomorrow morning,' said Tilly. 'Maybe you could knock on our door to make sure we don't oversleep?'

'Of course we can,' said Beryl, crossing with her sister to the door. 'What time would you like us?'

'We've got an appointment at St Kipper's at five.'

Betty laughed. 'Don't tell me you're digging someone up!'

'That's exactly what we're doing,' said Hettie, as she closed the door.

Chapter Twenty-Six

Poppa's van was already parked outside St Kipper's when Hettie, Bruiser and Tilly arrived. They had walked down the high street to the church in darkness and only now was there a slight promise of dawn as Hettie looked up at the church spire towering above them. The institution of the Church held no meaning for her but she marvelled at the glorious buildings that held so much history, all built on a foundation of faith – a faith that she found impossible to believe in. For her, the Church and its practitioners had lost their way.

St Kipper's had stood as a beacon of respectability at the bottom of the high street for over a hundred years and those buried in its hallowed ground had found safe harbour there. The town's notable dignitaries all slept within its confines; having laboured in life to achieve eternal peace, as they were lowered into the ground, they became just another headstone in the town's history.

Hettie loved churchyards, especially the wild ones where nature had clawed back the land set aside for burials. Best of all she loved the inscriptions on the stones, potted histories of lives lived well, or in some cases not so well. As she walked up the path that led to Horace Catberry's grave, it was with sadness that she noted the resting places of some of the cats she'd known personally; they were part of her own history and she couldn't help but wonder whether she herself might end her story here.

Morbid was the last to arrive, having parked her van further up the high street to avoid suspicion. Poppa and Bruiser had already begun the digging while Hettie and Tilly stood back to watch. 'Sorry I'm a bit late but I've only just got back from a removal,' Morbid said. 'In fact, Micky Strumshore is still in me van as I didn't have time to get him back to Shroud and Trestle but I don't think he'll mind. Looks like the digging is going well though.'

'What will we do when we get to the coffin?' asked Hettie, feeling slightly nervous. All she could see of Poppa and Bruiser now were the tops of their heads, as shovel after shovel of dirt was flung up into the air.

'Well, if all you want is the stuff out of the coffin, we can leave it in the ground and just take the lid off,' said Morbid, 'but it'll probably mean you getting down there with me.'

Hettie shuddered, showing that she clearly hadn't thought things through. 'You mean you want me to climb in on top of the coffin?'

'That's right,' said Morbid, 'but there's nothing to worry about. I promise you – that cat was very dead when I put him in his coffin so he won't bite.'

'We're there,' shouted Poppa. 'Do you want us to get the lid off?'

Hettie, Tilly and Morbid approached the hole and stared down into it. 'I'll take it from here,' said Morbid, offering a paw to Poppa as he clambered out, followed by Bruiser. Both cats were covered in soil and clay. They stood back, leaning on their spades, as Morbid lowered herself into the grave. Hettie was about to follow but Morbid raised her paw. 'Not just yet,' she said, pulling a screwdriver out of her coat pocket. 'This bit could be unpleasant so I advise you all to stand back because of the gas.'

Hettie looked puzzled and stayed to watch as Tilly retreated to stand by Poppa and Bruiser. Morbid went round the top of the coffin, releasing all the fastenings with the screwdriver. She pulled a large handkerchief out of her pocket and tied it over her nose and mouth before gently lifting the lid. There was a sudden rush of putrid air as the gas escaped from the coffin, forcing Hettie back to stand with Tilly. Morbid wrestled the lid off and propped it up in the grave. 'Ready when you are,' she said, 'but you'd better hurry up – it's getting light.'

Hettie returned to the graveside and stared down at the corpse of Horace Catberry, dressed in his Sunday best, with old copper pennies on his eyes. The body was surrounded by papers and bundles of letters. 'Thinking about it, it's not really a good idea for you to come down here,' said Morbid. 'He's a bit ripe, as they didn't want him embalmed, but I'll chuck the papers up to you.'

Hettie was greatly relieved at Morbid's suggestion and Tilly joined her to help catch the material. 'Do you want all of it?' asked Morbid. 'I think I stuck some of it under him but that stuff is going to be a bit messy and probably not readable.'

'Don't worry about those,' said Hettie, beginning to feel slightly sick. 'Just the papers you can get to easily will be fine.'

Morbid removed all the papers and letters from the top of the body, throwing them up to Hettie and Tilly. Hettie caught most of them as Tilly was completely distracted by the horror of Horace's corpse. She'd seen plenty of bodies during her work with Hettie but this was a whole new experience and one she hoped wouldn't be repeated.

'That's about it,' said Morbid, 'so I'm going to screw him down but before I do I just want to check something.' It was hard to see what Morbid was doing as she straddled the dead cat and Hettie gathered together the papers from the coffin and backed away from the grave with Tilly. Morbid concluded her business and put the coffin lid back into place, shutting the early morning light out for the last time on Horace Catberry. She secured the lid and heaved herself out of the grave, pleased to be back on firm ground. Poppa and Bruiser moved forward with their shovels and filled the grave in, replacing the simple wooden cross that bore Horace's name. Bruiser packed the turf around the grave, doing his best to make it look undisturbed and the five cats made their way out into the high street just as the sun rose in the sky, accompanied by the dawn chorus as the world around them renewed itself.

Poppa and Bruiser did their best to dust themselves off but the mud and clay stuck to them, which made Tilly giggle in spite of the sombre nature of the occasion. 'You two look like a couple of Mr Dickens's urchins from *Oliver Twist*,' she said.

'We certainly aren't going to ask for more,' said Poppa, scraping the clay off his sleeve with his claws. 'That was an experience I wouldn't want to repeat.'

'You get used to it,' said Morbid, 'although I'm pleased not to have done a full exhumation. That would have been a really messy job. I can confirm that there was no Mog Nob lodged in Horace Catberry's throat, though, so he may well have been murdered.'

'That's what you were doing down there with the body!' said Hettie. 'That's really good to know.'

'I'd better be off,' said Morbid. 'I can't keep poor old Micky Strumshore waiting much longer in me van. I hope you find the papers interesting and let me know if you find your killer – or killers.'

'We will,' said Hettie, 'and thank you for all your help. By the way, we think we've managed to identify the bodies in the vat. We think there might have been some sort of racket going on with Lockjaw Jarvis and the Catberrys.'

'Why doesn't that surprise me?' said Morbid. 'I don't know much about the Catberrys but old Lockjaw has a pretty bad reputation in undertaking circles. Anyway, bye for now.'

Morbid strode purposely up the high street towards her van and Poppa climbed into his, rolling his window down. 'I said I'd give Poppa a paw with a boiler this mornin' if yer don't need me,' said Bruiser, 'but I'll be back by lunchtime if that's OK?'

'Of course it is,' said Hettie. 'We've got plenty to keep us busy looking through all these papers and letters but we may need you to run us out to Catberry-on-the-Brink this afternoon.'

'Do you need a lift back to the bakery?' asked Poppa. 'We're going out that way?'

Hettie shook her head. 'No thank you. The walk will do us good, and after our Burk and Hair experience, I think fresh air is what we need – but thank you for your help and lunch is on me next time we're together at Bloomers.'

'Right'o,' said Poppa. 'I hope you find what you're looking for.'

Bruiser jumped into Poppa's van and the two cats drove off together, leaving Hettie and Tilly to make their way home under the weight of Horace Catberry's secrets.

Chapter Twenty-Seven

By the time Hettie and Tilly returned to the bakery, there was a hive of industry around the bread ovens as Betty and Beryl prepared their pies, breads and cakes for the day. The dawn chorus the sisters were offering was very different from the one Hettie and Tilly had experienced on their walk home. Beryl, who loved a musical, was offering her Gilbert and Sullivan medley, punctuated by Betty's renditions of some of her favourite hits from the sixties. The whole scene became incongruous when Hettie and Tilly stepped over the threshold with Horace Catberry's grave papers that didn't smell anywhere near as nice as the freshly baked bread that Beryl had just pulled out of one of the ovens.

'Whatever have you got there?' asked Betty, putting her paw up to her nose. 'Is that what you've been digging up?'

'Yes,' said Hettie. 'We're hoping that they might shed some light on Morgana's murder.'

'I don't know,' said Beryl. 'I never had you two down as grave robbers. Could you manage an egg and bacon bap each? I'm about to put my griddle on for the breakfast trade. Mind you, you'll have to give your paws a good wash after touching all those papers.'

'That would be lovely,' said Tilly. 'Grave robbing is hungry work.'

Beryl bustled off into the bakery with Betty and Hettie and Tilly let themselves into their room. Tilly fetched an old newspaper and spread it across their table. 'I think we'd better put all that stuff on here,' she said. 'It does smell quite nasty.'

'That's not surprising, considering where it's all been for the last few weeks,' said Hettie, 'and it's good to know that our suspicions were right about the Mog Nob.'

'If Horace was murdered, it all points to Praline,' said Tilly, washing her paws in the sink and drying them on the front of her cardigan.

'I'm hoping to find some clues that point to that in these papers,' said Hettie. 'She was obviously keen to hide something and it's the perfect way to bury evidence.'

'Unless someone comes along and digs it up,' said Tilly. 'Maybe that's why Horace wasn't put in the family mausoleum out at Sunny Tails. I suppose you can get at the coffins more easily in there than buried in the ground.'

'That's a good point,' said Hettie, rinsing her paws, 'and I'm wondering what will happen to the Catberry mausoleum if Lolly sells up. Mind you, if Lockjaw

Jarvis has had anything to do with it, half those coffins are probably empty.'

Beryl knocked on the door and came straight in, bearing two large egg and bacon baps and two frothy coffees. 'Get these while they're still nice,' she said. 'You don't want a congealed egg, do you? Nothing worse. Sister says your pies of the day are chicken and leek as she's trying out a new sauce and would value your opinions. I'll pop them in to you a bit later, in time for your suppers.'

The tradition of a free daily pie as part of Hettie and Tilly's rent had been established at a time when they had fallen down on their luck. Now it had become a token of kindness and one that they never took for granted. Living at the bakery gave them everything in life they could ever need, including a family that neither cat had had before – and having Bruiser at the bottom of the garden made all four female cats feel safe and secure.

After being sufficiently grateful they waved Beryl off. Hettie took her bap and her coffee to her armchair to get them as far away from Horace's papers as possible and Tilly settled down with her breakfast on her blanket. 'The sooner we get those papers read the better,' said Hettie. 'I don't think we can live with that smell for long.'

Tilly agreed and attacked her bap with great enthusiasm, ending up with most of the egg on her paws, face and even behind her ears. 'I think you'll be next for Betty and Beryl's twin-tub,' said Hettie.

Tilly giggled and padded to the sink for a cursory wash. 'I don't know how you manage to stay so clean,' she said, 'and half the fun of an egg and bacon bap is the mess.'

'You should know,' said Hettie. 'Come on – we can't put this off any longer. Let's take a look at this stuff so that we can get rid of it as soon as possible.'

Hettie and Tilly pulled their dining chairs up to the table and Tilly sorted the papers into two piles, one of letters and the other of papers and documents. 'I'll look at some of these letters if you want to see what these documents are,' she said.

There were two bundles of letters and Tilly started with the ones tied with blue ribbon. The top letter was addressed to Horace Catberry, care of Sunny Tails, and was dated the twentieth of December. Tilly scanned it quickly before deciding to read it out loud to Hettie.

'I think this might be what we're looking for. No wonder Praline wanted to bury it.

"My Dearest Horace,

I've been trying to talk to you for days, but Praline seems to be everywhere and Pettifur is so suffocating. I have some news but I'm not sure you'll be pleased. I am expecting kittens and they are yours. For me, this is the best news but I know it makes things really difficult for you. Maybe we could meet at Sunny Tails to talk things through?

I miss you very much.

Morgana X".'

'That all seems very straightforward,' said Hettie, 'as long as she was telling the truth. Are there any letters dated after that one?'

Tilly worked through the bundle, checking the dates as Hettie picked up a small and rather badly stained book. 'This must be the recipe book that Morbid mentioned. It has Horace Catberry's nameplate on the inside cover, and just look at this – it's the recipe for The Tabby in Black chocolate. It's an odd thing to bury Horace with if they intended to continue with it.'

Hettie traced the list of ingredients with her claw. 'There's nothing remarkable about this, just lots of cocoa, sugar and milk in huge quantities, as you'd expect.' Hettie flicked through the rest of the pages, featuring several different paw writings over the years, until she came to the back of the book. There was a list of dates, batch numbers and names going back over four years but it was the most recent one that caught her eye. 'Look at this,' she said. 'The last entry was for the twenty-fifth of November last year. It says Verity Tinker and the ones before that are roughly a year apart: Caramela Catberry, Edward Seeker and Finch Seeker.'

'The bodies in the vat,' said Tilly. 'Edward must be Ned, Perks' and Sparks' uncle, and their father was Finch. Florrie was right to say that those spectacles belonged to Caramela Catberry, Pettifur's first wife and Dandy and Grace's mother.'

'Now we know why this book was buried with Horace – he was obviously putting the bodies into the chocolate to enhance The Tabby in Black selection,' said Hettie. 'That's a truly awful secret to take to your grave. If Praline found out about her sister Verity being disposed of in the vat and Horace's affair with Morgana, she had more than enough reasons to bump him off and bury his sins with him.'

'These letters make it very clear that Morgana and Horace were seeing each other long before Morgana married poor old Pettifur,' said Tilly. 'This one is when Morgana was on her honeymoon. She says she can't bear to be away from Horace and wishes they could come home sooner. She says Pettifur is the most boring cat on earth.'

Hettie shook her head. 'What an awful mess – and so many victims, one way or another, if you think about it. Praline was just protecting her family by burying all this stuff with Horace. No wonder she paid us to take our paws off the handlebars. She must have been horrified when she found out that Pettifur had called us in to start digging around. Are there any later dates on those letters? I'd love to know what Horace's reaction was to finding out that Morgana was expecting his kittens.'

'Nothing after the one I read out so I suppose they met up to discuss the situation but we may never know what they decided – Pettifur obviously didn't know about it when he called us in.'

'Maybe he does now,' said Hettie. 'Perhaps Praline came clean to him about what she knew in their meeting on Saturday morning. If she'd read these letters, she'd know all about Horace and Morgana's deceit, and if she passed that on to Pettifur it would give him the strongest of motives for murdering Morgana and her kittens. If they'd been born, they would have threatened his inheritance.'

'So what do we do now?' asked Tilly, tying the bundle of letters back together.

'As we have these papers, we should go through them to see if there's anything else of importance. There'll have to be a showdown with Praline and Pettifur, but we must get our facts straight before we venture into that territory, and all this is going to come as a terrible shock to the rest of the family. In hindsight, they were right to be suspicious of Morgana, but imagine how she must have felt when Horace died. He left her out on a limb with a family who hated her, a husband she didn't love and a dead cat's kittens on the way. I'm surprised she didn't shrink-wrap herself with all that to deal with.'

Tilly pulled some of the papers towards her and started going through them. 'A lot of this stuff is about The Tabby in Black selection,' she said. 'Sales figures, graphs and thank you notes from shops. Judging by the look of this graph, the figures started rising four years ago.'

'At the same time as Horace started putting bodies in the chocolate,' said Hettie. 'He was certainly on to a winner but fancy including his own relatives! You couldn't make it up.'

'Well, it is supposed to be a family business,' said Tilly, being unusually sarcastic.

'Ah,' said Hettie, unfolding one of the more substantial documents, 'this should be good – it's Horace's will and it's dated the first of January this year, so not long before he died. It starts by revoking all previous wills and it's very straightforward: he leaves his entire fortune, business, lands and properties to Morgana Catberry and her immediate descendants. Then there's a list of all his properties, including Catberry Manor House, Sunny Tails Retirement Home, The Brink public house and cottages numbers one to twenty in Catberry-on-the-Brink. It also mentions the Catberry Chocolate and Biscuit factory and all supporting premises.'

'No wonder Praline wanted that buried with him,' said Tilly. 'I don't suppose Morgana ever saw that will, unless he told her what he was going to do.'

'I don't know whether to admire Horace or think he's the meanest cat who ever created a bar of chocolate,' said Hettie, carefully folding the will. 'The big question is what do we do about it? There must be a will that left the business to Pettifur and the various inheritances to other members of the family, and Praline decided to use that after Horace's death, but technically it's Morgana's next of kin who should inherit the lot. I can see why that five hundred pounds that Praline gave us was just small change compared with the Catberry fortune going elsewhere.'

'As Morgana is dead, it seems only right that the Catberrys inherit everything,' said Tilly. 'It seems wrong to pass it all on to a stranger in Morgana's family.'

'I agree,' said Hettie, 'but we're between the devil and the not-so-deep blue sea – more like muddied waters. Horace's last wish was that Morgana and her kittens should inherit everything whether Praline liked it or not; subsequently, Praline may have discovered this new will and murdered Horace, and one of the other members of the family may have decided to remove Morgana altogether – so we're back to square one with the suspects list.'

'One thing's for sure – I can't stand this smell any longer,' said Tilly, looking in the middle drawer of the filing cabinet, where she kept her plastic bags. 'I'm going to put all that stuff in this until we decide what to do with it.'

As Tilly was forcing the letters and documents into a large plastic bag, the telephone rang in the sideboard. She abandoned her task to answer it, as Hettie filled the kettle to make a milky tea. 'The No. 2 Feline Detective Agency, Tilly speaking, how may I help?' she said, in her business voice. 'Oh, hello Grace, thank you for getting in touch. What's that? But that's terrible – I'm so sorry. Yes, of course we can. How about Bloomers at one o'clock?'

Tilly looked shocked as she replaced the receiver. 'That was Grace. She said Pettifur has driven a Creamy Egg car into one of the factory walls and killed himself and for some unknown reason he's left a letter addressed to us which she's bringing to Bloomers at lunchtime.'

Chapter Twenty-Eight

Bloomers was quiet for a Wednesday and Grace Catberry was waiting at Hettie and Tilly's usual table when they arrived. She was hugging a hot chocolate in her paws and staring into space looking totally desolate.

Hettie ordered two milky teas from Dolly as they made their way across to the table. Tilly slid in beside Grace and Hettie sat opposite, both lost for words. Grace broke the silence by pushing a letter across the table. 'Pops left this for you and I was hoping that it might explain why he killed himself.' Grace lapsed into uncontrolled sobbing as if she'd been holding it back for some time. Tilly moved to comfort her, as Dolly rushed over with a pawful of tissues.

Hettie stared down at the letter, turning it in her paws and trying to decide whether to open it in front of Grace, knowing that if she did she would have to share the contents with her. Instead she decided to find out what had happened to Pettifur and how the family had responded. Grace eventually stopped crying and Hettie seized her opportunity. 'I know this is all so painful,' she said. 'When someone kills themselves it's the cats left behind who suffer the most, as there are so many unanswered questions – but to help us understand maybe you could tell us what happened?'

'It's really quite simple,' said Grace. 'We all had breakfast together this morning and afterwards he just left, saying he was going to check on the factory. Dandy decided to go over about half an hour later to check on her Easter egg stocks and found him. He'd driven a Creamy Egg car into one of the factory walls. Dandy said it was really smashed up – he didn't stand a chance.'

Grace began to sob again, this time more quietly, and Hettie and Tilly let her as they sipped the milky teas that Dolly had just delivered. 'I'm sorry,' said Grace, trying hard to pull herself together, 'but I just can't get my head round what's happened. Why would he do that to us? And in such a violent way? Dandy's in bits. She's locked herself in her room and she won't come out. She saw him after the crash. She said he was all messed up and there was so much blood.'

'That must have been terrible for her,' said Tilly, 'but it sounds like he didn't suffer – and sometimes, when life gets too much, it can be a peaceful way out, but you and Dandy have your lives before you and you will come to terms with this in time.'

'Where did he leave this letter?' asked Hettie.

'He gave it to Sparks on his way out this morning. Sparks put it with the rest of the post on the plate by the door. As you can see it's marked very urgent and when Sparks found out what had happened to Pops he gave it to me. I was going to open it but Dandy said I shouldn't and that I should bring it straight to you. Then she locked herself in her room.'

'And does your grandmother or anyone else know about the letter?'

Grace shook her head. 'No. She's shut herself away with Lolly and Oliver and Rhubarb are dealing with the crash at the factory. They've called in your friend Morbid to take Pops away.'

Grace's voice faltered as once again the tears fell, this time silently, and Tilly's thoughts went back to Saturday night and the sheer joy that Grace and Dandy had shared as they cavorted across the stage, delivering their music. Now Grace looked small and very vulnerable and her sister would replay the horror of Pettifur's death over and over again as his suicide engulfed them both and robbed them of any happy memories they could have shared with him in the future.

'Aren't you going to read his letter?' asked Grace. 'It might explain why he's done this and Dandy and I do need to know.'

'I think it best to leave things for today,' said Hettie. 'You and Dandy have more than enough to cope with at the moment. Right now, your sister needs you. We'll get in touch if there's anything in the letter that's important to you both, I promise.'

'I suppose you're right,' said Grace, getting to her feet, 'but why didn't he leave us a letter? Or even say goodbye?' she said, suddenly raising her voice. 'He just walked out after breakfast and was gone for ever. What do we do now? Thanks to him checking out early, we're lumbered with inheriting the family business – which seems to be in shreds – and giving up everything we love to keep the Catberrys afloat.'

Grace was beginning to feel angry and Hettie thought that was a good sign under the circumstances. She suspected that Pettifur's letter was some sort of confession and his daughters may well have mixed feelings about their father once they knew the truth, but for now they should mourn him. 'Why don't you give us a call tomorrow?' she suggested. 'Maybe we could meet up with you and Dandy to have a proper talk about all this? I think it's all a bit raw at the moment and it sounds like you both have a lot to come to terms with. Just make sure that no one from the family bullies you into anything you may both regret in the future.'

'You mean Oliver and Rhubarb?' said Grace. 'Don't worry, they won't be getting their paws on anything Pops left to us.'

'I'm pleased to hear it,' said Hettie. 'Now, go and comfort your sister and we'll talk tomorrow.'

'Thank you,' said Grace, then turned and walked slowly to the door and out into the high street.

'Poor Grace,' said Tilly. 'I wonder what Pettifur has to say for himself? I can't wait to find out.'

'Well, you'll have to,' said Hettie, 'because I'm starving and here comes Dolly with the menus.'

'That cat looked a bit upset,' said Dolly. 'Didn't they get the support tour with the Travellin' Whoopsies? Because if they didn't they was robbed.'

'No, nothing like that,' said Tilly. 'Grace and Dandy's father killed himself this morning.'

'Oh my goodness!' exclaimed Dolly. 'No wonder she didn't drink 'er 'ot chocolate! How did he do it?'

'As far as we know, he drove a car into a brick wall,' said Hettie.

'Not a great way to go,' said Dolly. 'In Cornwall, we prefer to jump off cliffs – much less mess, and if you're lucky you get a burial at sea as well, unless the tide brings you in, of course. Anyway, we've a ham and cheese omelette, a chicken curry with rice and poppadums or a fish pie on the specials – or anything you fancy from the menu.'

'I'll have the curry,' said Hettie, 'with a few chips to dip in.'

'And I'll have the same,' said Tilly, passing the menus back to Dolly.

'What can I get you for your puddin's?'

'Sadly I don't think we have time today,' said Hettie, 'but the curry will be lovely.'

Dolly disappeared into the kitchen with their order and returned within minutes with the curries. 'There you go,' she said, 'that should turn your ears pink if it doesn't blow your head off first. Molly 'asn't stinted on 'er 'ot madras – made me eyes water when she asked me to stir it. I'll just fetch your poppadums and the chips. You'll need them to take the heat off a bit.'

Dolly was right to give a warning, as the curry was very hot, but Hettie and Tilly cleared their plates in record time, taking Pettifur's letter back to their room at the bakery to read in private. The smell of Horace's grave papers still hung in the air so Tilly threw their small window open to let some fresh air in and the two cats settled down at their table to read the letter.

Hettie slit the envelope open with her claw and pulled out two sheets of blue headed notepaper. Both were paw written and covered both sides and the letter was signed by Pettifur. 'This is quite some suicide note,' said Hettie, 'or a detailed confession, of course. Let's see what he has to say. It's dated today so he obviously wrote it this morning.

"Dear Miss Bagshot and Miss Jenkins,

When you read this I shall be at peace, although I know that my sins will follow me to my grave, and it is right that they should. As you and Miss Jenkins are strangers to me, I feel able to be honest with you about the terrible thing I have done; had I lived, I know that you would have eventually faced me with my crime. I am not a cold-blooded murderer but I did kill Morgana – and that is more than I can bear, especially because of the cruel way in which I killed her. In my own defence, I need to explain the events that led up to that terrible moment.

"I knew when I married her that she didn't love me and I also suspected that another cat was in her life, but I stupidly didn't realise who that cat was. I honestly thought that things would get better for us and she did seem to be settling down and taking part in family matters and trying to carve out a role for herself. She hated the idea of the factory but she loved working with the residents at Sunny Tails, which I was really pleased to see, but now I know it was just a smokescreen for what was really happening there.

"Last Saturday morning, after my mother announced that she was closing the factory, I went to her rooms to plead with her to let me take control of everything as my father had wished, or to let me and Morgana leave the family to start a new life somewhere else. She got very angry and told me she'd discovered some letters written by Morgana to my father, making it clear that they had been seeing each other for some time and that they'd been meeting up at Sunny Tails. I asked to see the letters, but she told me she'd buried them with my father along with a new will he'd made leaving everything to Morgana and the rest of the family without a penny. I told her I didn't believe her and she told me to go and ask Morgana if it was true. That's what I intended on doing but as I was leaving her rooms she told me that Morgana was expecting kittens and that they were my father's. That's why he had changed his will.

"I left her rooms in a blind rage and threw myself into closing the factory with Oliver but what my mother had told me was eating away at me. I spent the afternoon in the office, staring at some sales figures, not knowing what to do, but I realised that I would have to confront Morgana so I went back to the Manor to find her. She wasn't in her room so I left her a note saying that I had something important to discuss with her and I asked her to meet me at the factory at a quarter past eight that evening. I went to the library and waited until I saw her walking down the drive. I locked the library door and went out through the French windows, carrying one of my father's walking sticks, and followed her to the factory. I was possessed: as soon as she turned towards me, I lost control. I sprang at her knocking her to the ground with my stick and dragged her into the loading bay. I tied her paws and feet and she began to cry, so I hit her again and fed her onto the rollers of the shrink-wrapper. She just kept crying like á wounded animal and I just wanted her to be quiet, so I started the machine and turned it to maximum heat and suddenly it was over and she lay bound up and still. I left the machine running and left her there. I went out by the staff entrance, avoiding the night watch cat who was about to come on duty, and made my way back to the library, entering through the French windows. I unlocked the door and waited for Sparks to bring me a drink, which he always did around ten o'clock. Grace and Dandy called in to say goodnight around one and the night watch cat called me after that to say the shrink-wrapper had been left on. I went back to the factory and pretended to discover the body and then I called you.

"As the hours passed, I began to realise what I had done and the impact it would have on Grace and Dandy if they found out. My father had cheated me and I had done the same to them, and I just couldn't live with that. It is my last wish that you make sure my daughters are treated fairly by the family. My mother has buried my father's last will with him and I hope that the original will stand so that Grace and Dandy will inherit everything that I possessed in life – and that in time they will forgive me for what I've done.

Pettifur Catberry"

'So there we are,' said Hettie. 'You couldn't ask for a more comprehensive confession and what's really annoying is we'd almost worked it out, but it seems to me that Praline Catberry has a lot to answer for. Whether she likes it or not, it's time she came clean about Horace's death and she needs to know that she's also indirectly responsible for Morgana's murder and her own son's suicide.'

'But we're banned from the Manor so how do we get to her?' asked Tilly. 'I doubt she'll see us, and even if we do get to see her she can easily deny everything that Pettifur has said in that letter.'

'Not if we dangle that carrier bag of Horace's grave letters in front of her nose. Then there's the issue of the bodies in the chocolate – I'd like to hear her side of

234

things about that. We still haven't entirely got to the bottom of what was happening at Sunny Tails either, but it all needs to come out before we can call it case closed. I think if Bruiser is back from his plumbing job with Poppa, we'll ask him to run us out to Sunny Tails this afternoon – and as an extra treat, we'll call in on Praline Catberry on our way home.'

Chapter Twenty-Nine

Sunny Tails was by no means as peaceful as on Hettie and Tilly's last visit. A whole group of residents had gathered outside the front entrance as Bruiser drove Miss Scarlet into the car park. 'I wonder what's going on here?' said Hettie, sliding the lid back on the sidecar.

'Maybe they're gathering for one of their activities,' said Tilly, 'although it's a bit late in the day to be going anywhere.'

'Let's go and find out,' said Hettie. 'Perhaps Lolly Catberry has given them their marching orders earlier than expected.'

Bruiser transferred himself to the sidecar to sit in the sun and read his paper as Hettie and Tilly headed for the front of the building. The old gardener they'd met before was there and Tilly approached him. 'What's happening?' she asked, looking round at the rest of the residents, who all appeared quite agitated.

'Biscuit Florrie's gone missin',' he said, sucking on his clay pipe. 'She was s'posed ta talk ta that newspaper cat from the *Daily Snout* about us bein' closed down by Miss Lolly but we can't find 'er an' 'er bed's not bin slept in.'

'Maybe she's gone to visit friends?' suggested Hettie.

The gardener shook his head. 'No, not Biscuit Florrie. She wouldn't miss out on a chance to save Sunny Tails. She stood up ta Miss Lolly yesterdee – told 'er straight, she did, at the meetin', as 'ow Mr Sylvester set this place up an' how Miss Lolly had no right ta sell up.'

Alarm bells began to ring in Hettie's ears, especially after the note the Butters had passed on to them; the word 'compost' kept coming into her mind. 'Come on,' she said, tugging Tilly's arm, 'we're going to pay a visit to Lockjaw Jarvis.'

Bruiser leapt out of the sidecar as Hettie and Tilly returned to Miss Scarlet. 'Florrie's gone missing,' said Hettie. 'I have a hunch that Lockjaw Jarvis might be able to help, if it's not too late.'

The three cats sped off on the motorbike, past a row of terraced houses, stopping at the end of the street where Lockjaw Jarvis's furniture shop stood. It was more of a front room than a shop, and gave the appearance of inactivity as Hettie stared through the filthy window at a few pieces of unfinished woodwork. To the side of the property, there was a rather dilapidated old van and a gate leading into the backyard.

'Tha's where that oven is an' them coffins,' said Bruiser, pointing his paw at the gate, 'but it don't look like 'e's about.'

Hettie bustled forward and opened the gate. The yard was as Bruiser had described it but there was no sign of Lockjaw. She called out, hoping for a response from the house, but there was only silence. She went deeper into the yard, as Tilly and Bruiser watched from the gate, and called out again. This time she was rewarded by a frantic banging coming from a shed next to the oven.

'There's something going on in there!' she shouted to Bruiser. 'It's padlocked so we'll have to break in.'

Bruiser responded by taking up an axe that was lying on a pile of logs and with one swift blow broke the lock in half. Hettie, Tilly and Bruiser piled into the shed to be met by a row of coffins but only one of them had a lid on it and that was where the banging was coming from.

The three cats pounced on the coffin, unscrewing the brass fixings until the lid could be lifted. There inside, looking tear-stained and dishevelled, was Florrie Bundee. She used the last of her strength to leap out of the coffin into Bruiser's arms and clung to him, shaking. Her escape was short-lived, as a shadow fell across the open door of the shed. Hettie turned to see a cat wielding the axe Bruiser had used to break the lock and snarling as he came towards them. Bruiser unceremoniously deposited Florrie on the floor and sprang at the cat, knocking him into the side of one of the coffins. Hettie, realising that the danger was far from over, grabbed Florrie from the floor and with

Tilly's help got her out into the yard, leaving Bruiser to deal with the cat she assumed was Lockjaw Jarvis.

It didn't take long for Bruiser to get the better of his opponent. Having wrestled the axe off him, he knocked him to the floor with one of the coffin lids. Lockjaw knew he was beaten and pleaded for mercy. Bruiser pulled the cat to his feet and marched him out into the yard. 'What would you like me ta do with 'im?'

'I'd like a little chat with him,' said Hettie, 'but I think Tilly should take Florrie to sit in Miss Scarlet while we do that.'

Tilly nodded and took Florrie's arm but she broke free and swiped Lockjaw across his face, drawing blood; then she did it again, leaving Lockjaw cowering in front of her with his paws protecting his head from any further blows. 'If I had my way I'd bury you alive in one of your coffins,' said Florrie. 'You're an evil cat and I won't forget what you did to me.'

Florrie returned to Tilly and both cats left the yard, leaving Hettie and Bruiser to have a conversation with the cat in front of them. 'I'd like to talk to you about Sunny Tails,' said Hettie. 'We can do that here or we could go inside your house where it might be more comfortable?'

Lockjaw grunted and limped to his back door. Hettie and Bruiser followed him into a small and very disorganised kitchen. There was a table in the centre of the room, covered in dirty plates and half-eaten food; the sink was piled high with dishes and, although there were three chairs in the room, they were all broken, which Hettie thought didn't say much for Lockjaw's furniture-making skills.

'I suppose we ought to start with why you shut one of the Sunny Tails residents in a coffin,' said Hettie, 'especially as she was clearly alive at the time.'

'I was just doin' as I was told,' said Lockjaw. 'I was told ta teach 'er a lesson by Miss Lolly as she was causin' trouble an' needed shuttin' up.'

'And do you do everything the Catberrys tell you to do?'

'If they pays I do.'

'Does that include messing around with dead bodies that should have been buried or cremated?'

'Maybe it does, maybe it doesn't. I just do as I'm told, no questions asked. I don't do no 'arm – you can't do no 'arm if they're dead.'

'And how long have you been helping the Catberrys with their dead?'

''Bout four years,' said Lockjaw. 'Mr Horace came ta me and said 'e was interested in preservin' some of them old cats at Sunny Tails after they was dead. 'E 'ad me deliver some bodies to 'is factory, where 'e said 'e 'ad some special stuff ta put 'em in. I just did the job an' 'e paid up an' that was that.'

'How many bodies did you deliver to the factory?'

Lockjaw scratched his head before replying. 'Three or four, maybe. There was one a bit before Christmas – ginger cat, worked in them kitchens at Sunny

Tails. They all came from there except one – pretty little corpse, she was. 'Ad an accident at the factory. Mr Horace paid double for that one an' she's got a coffin over at the mausoleum – empty, of course.'

'Let's get back to Miss Lolly and the poor cat you shut in the coffin,' said Hettie. 'Were you going to leave her there to die?'

'Course not,' said Lockjaw, rather indignantly. 'What do yer take me for? I'm no killer. I was just puttin' the frighteners on 'er, tha's all.'

'Did you put a threatening note under her door?'

Lockjaw laughed. 'You mean about turnin' 'er into compost?'

'Yes, that's exactly what I mean,' said Hettie.

'As far as my old eyes can see, there was no 'arm done, an' if you've got a problem with that you should be talkin' ta Miss Lolly, but don't say I sent yer.'

Hettie realised that she'd gathered all the information she was going to get out of Lockjaw Jarvis so she brought the conversation to an end with a warning. 'Florrie threatened you with the prospect of burying you alive,' she said. 'If I hear of any more malpractice regarding burials or cremations, Bruiser here and I will personally dig the hole to put you in – and that's a promise.'

Without another word, Hettie swept out of the kitchen, followed by Bruiser, leaving Lockjaw Jarvis with a lot to think about.

Bruiser drove Miss Scarlet triumphantly into the car park at Sunny Tails, with Hettie riding pillion and

Tilly and Florrie waving from the sidecar as the cats from the retirement home gathered round, delighted to see Florrie safely returned to them. 'You must all come in for afternoon tea,' said Florrie, as Bruiser helped her out of the sidecar. 'I owe you a huge debt of gratitude. Another hour in that hateful coffin and I'm sure I would have died.'

Much as Hettie would have loved to join Florrie for afternoon tea with Tilly and Bruiser, there were more pressing matters, and the smell of Horace Catberry's grave papers coming from Bruiser's top box reminded her that the final showdown with Praline was their next objective. 'We're so pleased that we found you in time,' she said, climbing into the sidecar next to Tilly, 'and we'd love to come for tea another day but we have business at Catberry Manor and it won't wait.'

Chapter Thirty

Sparks barely had a chance to open the door before Hettie and Tilly pushed past him. 'We've come to see Miss Praline and Miss Lolly,' said Hettie, 'and it's urgent.'

'I'm afraid Miss Praline is not to be disturbed,' said Sparks. 'Mr Pettifur died this morning and, as you can imagine, the family is in deep mourning.'

'Yes, I know all about that, but we have some very important documents in this bag that Miss Praline needs to see and it won't wait,' said Hettie, waving Tilly's carrier bag in front of Sparks's nose.

The butler took a step back as the smell filled his nostrils, but he was convinced by Hettie's insistence that Praline Catberry had to be disturbed. 'Miss Praline is with Miss Lolly up in her rooms. I'll show you up to her.'

'No need,' said Hettie, already on the bottom step of the staircase, 'we know the way.' The two cats bounded up the stairs, leaving the butler to stare after them. Hettie hesitated briefly at the door to Praline's rooms and lifted her paw to knock, then changed her mind and barged straight in, followed closely by Tilly and her offensive bag.

The scene before them reminded Tilly of one the TV adaptations of Miss Austen's *Sense and Stupidity*. Praline Catberry lay on a chaise longue in a substantial bay window, bathed in sunshine and staring tearfully across the Manor's formal gardens, while Lolly sat on a small stool next to her, reading a poem from a collection by Porkshire author and poet Emmerline Bronte. Both cats looked startled by such a forceful intrusion, and Emmerline was cut off in the middle of one of her most meaningful stanzas as Praline protested, knocking the poetry book out of Lolly's paws. 'How dare you enter my rooms in such a way!' she shouted. 'And today of all days, when my poor son lies dead. I thought I had made myself very clear about my business with you being concluded.'

'Yes, you made that very clear,' said Hettie, 'but our business with you is far from over. You've no one to blame but yourself for Pettifur's death but we'll get to that shortly. I'd like to talk to Miss Lolly first.'

'And I'd like you to leave immediately,' said Praline. 'My daughter has no more to say to you than I have, so kindly leave before I call Sparks to eject you forcibly.'

'If we're going to involve Sparks in our conversation, perhaps we should discuss why Horace Catberry decided to include his father and uncle as a vital ingredient in The Tabby in Black chocolate?' said Hettie.

Praline looked slightly deflated and gave Lolly a shove. 'You'd better speak to them,' she said, 'and then perhaps we can be left in peace.'

'Thank you,' said Hettie, turning her attention to Lolly. 'I just wanted to know why you thought it appropriate to have a resident at Sunny Tails locked in a coffin?'

Praline shot a look at her daughter but said nothing. 'I don't know what you mean,' said Lolly. 'Why would I do that?'

'I think it's probably up to me to ask the questions,' said Hettie, 'but if you're struggling with an answer, I can help. I gather you've given the residents notice to quit their homes at Sunny Tails because for some misguided reason you think you've inherited it from Morgana, or even Pettifur. I think your mother will be able to put you right on that one. However, you met with some understandable resistance at the meeting you called yesterday from Florrie Bundee, so you paid Lockjaw Jarvis to threaten, abduct and incarcerate her in a coffin. Mr Lockjaw was happy to confirm this when we paid him a visit this afternoon and, before you ask, we have returned Florrie to Sunny Tails – a little worse for her experience but thankfully alive.'

Lolly had no time to respond as her mother dealt a resounding blow to the back of her head, forcing her forward off the stool and leaving her dazed and spreadeagled on the very expensive Persian rug. 'You stupid girl!' said Praline. 'How much more grief do I have to take from this family? I wash my paws of the lot of you. Now go to your room and stay there.'

Lolly didn't need telling twice. She staggered to her feet, rubbing the back of her head, and fled from the room.

'I can see that you are not as easily dismissed,' said Praline, addressing Hettie and Tilly, 'but you must forgive Lolly – she is prone to dark moods and has been a difficult cat to raise. Her father's death has had a terrible effect on her and it has made her irrational.'

'It's not for us to forgive,' said Hettie, 'but I doubt that Florrie Bundee will forgive her for attempting to have her buried alive. That's some dark mood, if you don't mind my saying so.'

Praline sighed, as if bored with the conversation, and put her paw to her head. 'I'm afraid I can't cope with any more trouble today, so please say what you came to say and leave me in peace to grieve for my son.'

Hettie waved the carrier bag under Praline's nose before spilling its contents onto the rug that Lolly had so recently vacated. Praline stared at the familiar bundle of papers in disbelief, searching for a response, but any form of words escaped her.

'You obviously recognise these items,' said Hettie. 'We have looked through them and appreciate why you might have wanted to bury them with your late husband, but I think you owe it to your family and to us to tell the truth about Horace's death, his will and Morgana's murder.'

'So you have both come here to sit in judgement on me for what I had to do to protect my family?

When you've proved yourselves to be little more than grubby grave robbers?' said Praline trying desperately to maintain her icy composure.

'We haven't robbed anything,' said Hettie. 'As you can see, we've brought it all back to you, including Horace's latest will. We completely understand why you might have wanted to ignore the fact that he'd left everything to Morgana, but that is what he did. Technically, on Morgana's death, unless she made a will, the inheritance should have passed to her husband Pettifur, but as he's no longer with us, it surely must now revert back to Grace and Dandy, his heirs, unless Morgana has any relatives who may crawl out of the woodwork to contest it. That means that Lolly has no claim on Sunny Tails, other than a few shares, and the rest of the family are at the mercy of Grace and Dandy – and that includes you.'

'My granddaughters will do as I say,' said Praline. 'I won't see this family torn apart by Horace's indiscretions. That is why I buried them with him. He was the love of my life and I can never forgive him for making a fool of all of us.'

Praline's voice faltered as her haughty demeanour was replaced by a genuine sorrow and she fought to hold back her tears.

'So when did you find out about him and Morgana?'

'I had my suspicions for some time but on the day he died I found the letters from her in his desk drawer in the library and I faced him with them. He became very agitated and upset and started clutching his chest. I thought he was putting it on but then he started gasping for breath. I was so angry with him that I just watched as his life ebbed away and I should tell you now that I have no regrets about watching him die. When I found those letters something inside me died and my first thought was to protect the family. They all loved Horace, as I did, and I didn't want them to think badly of him so I buried him with his infidelity and the will that left everything to Morgana. I made up the story about him choking to make his death look like a tragic accident.'

'And what about the recipe book for The Tabby in Black chocolate?' asked Hettie. 'Did you realise what he'd been doing?'

'Only after he'd died. I was going through his papers and saw the names in the back of the book, including my sister Verity and my daughter-in-law Caramela. I assumed the bodies would just dissolve – it didn't even occur to me that they would be found until Oliver and Pettifur discovered them in the chocolate vat and you were called in to investigate. I was horrified that the truth would come out so that's why I closed the factory and paid you off.'

'And what about Pettifur? Why did you decide to tell him the truth?'

The mention of her dead son finally released the tears that Praline had denied herself and she sobbed her response. 'Because he was so angry with me for closing the factory. I lashed out at him, telling him about Horace and Morgana and the kittens. I never expected him to kill her, or himself.'

'So you knew that he'd murdered Morgana?'

'Not at first. He seemed so upset about discovering her body, but in the last couple of days he'd changed, as though his spirit had left him. He was just going about the Manor in a detached sort of way, like the rest of us didn't exist, which wasn't like him at all. None of the rest of the family got on with Morgana, but as far as I could see only Pettifur had a real reason for killing her after what I'd told him. When Dandy came and told me what he'd done this morning, I wasn't surprised – just heartbroken that it was me who had set him on his path of self-destruction.'

Hettie allowed Praline to collect herself briefly before continuing on the subject of Pettifer's suicide letter.

'He left a full confession, addressed to us, which Grace delivered earlier today. She has no idea what is in it,' said Hettie, 'so you must decide what you're going to tell the rest of the family.' She pulled the suicide note out of her pocket and gave it to Praline.

She clutched it to her but made no attempt to read it, reaching out to Hettie in her moment of despair.

'But what about all these things?' asked Praline, pointing to the documents on the rug. 'Should I share them with the family?'

Hettie shook her head. 'They were dead and buried once, so I suggest you cremate them this time. We have no further business here as long as you make sure that Grace and Dandy inherit everything, which – as you will see – was Pettifur's last wish. What you choose to tell them is up to you.'

Hettie and Tilly turned towards the door but Praline called them back. 'Wait!' she said. 'Am I to understand that you're willing to take these matters no further and that the conversation we have just had stays in this room?'

Hettie nodded. 'Yes, that's right. It's clear to both me and Tilly that there are many victims and no winners in this case, and we completely understand the situation you find yourself in, but we hope you will find a way of bringing your fractured family back together and allowing Grace and Dandy to take you all into the future. We will be returning the money you paid us for our silence and sending a bill for the work we have done.'

'There's no need to return the cheque,' said Praline. 'I have seen the error of my ways and I am more grateful to you than you could ever know for your discretion in these very painful matters. You are worth every penny.'

'It's all part of the service,' said Hettie.

'Thank you,' said Praline, through a veil of grateful tears.

Chapter Thirty-One

Spring had morphed into summer before Hettie and Tilly heard any more from the Catberry family. It was on one very hot day in the middle of June that Grace and Dandy decided to pay a call on them and found them relaxing in the Butters' garden just before tea.

'We hoped we'd catch you at home,' said Grace, appearing from the alleyway that led into the back-yard, swiftly followed by her sister. 'We thought you might like to hear our news.'

Bruiser, who'd been dozing in the sun by his shed, responded to the visitors by setting up two more deck-chairs as Grace and Dandy joined Hettie and Tilly in the shade of Betty's cherry tree.

'How lovely to see you both,' said Tilly, 'and just in time for tea. We were only wondering the other day what had happened to you all when we read in the *Daily Snout* about your tour with the Travelling Whoopsies.'

'Yeah, that was mega,' said Dandy, 'and we're recording an album in the autumn now we have our own studio.'

'I'm so pleased for you both,' said Hettie, shading her eyes with her paw from the sun. 'I hope it does really well for you. You deserve it. So where is your studio?'

'Well, that's part of our news,' said Grace. 'As you probably know, Pops left everything to us but we decided that we needed to do things differently as far as the family and the factory were concerned, so we formed a workers co-operative to give all the cats who were loyal to us a stake in the business. It's really put up productivity.'

'And how did that go down with the family?' asked Hettie.

'Not very well,' said Dandy. 'Oliver and Rhubarb were furious and quit. They've gone to America to work in the management of Solomon's Candy Clump, a factory set up by our great, great, great-uncle. We bought out Rhubarb's biscuit shares. Granny Praline has gone to live at Sunny Tails and is really happy there. She's taken up gardening and says that raising flowers is much nicer than keeping us Catberrys on the straight and narrow. But that left us rattling around in Catberry Manor with only Aunt Lolly to keep us company so the big news is that we've turned the whole place over to a residential recording and rehearsal studio. We funded all the studio gear by selling out our top biscuit lines to McKitties. We still live there but it's great to see the place being used for creative stuff rather than a family at war. Dire Streaks is booked in for sessions next week, which are beyond cool.'

Since leaving Praline to her grief, it had bothered Hettie that the case, although solved, had reached no conclusions regarding the complicated relationships within the family, but now she was satisfied that Grace and Dandy had steered the ship out of stormy waters with youthful flair and a sizeable helping of common sense.

'And what about Lolly?' asked Tilly.

'She's cheered up no end,' said Grace, 'so we've given her the job of booking all the bands into the studio and looking after them. We haven't had any of her dark moods since she took the job. Sparks and Perks have stayed on to help run the place and we've completely shut down the biscuit division to concentrate on only chocolate. We've got lots of new lines coming out for Christmas but we thought we'd bring you this, which is still top secret. We like to think it's the next generation of Catberry chocolate.'

Grace pulled a box out of her shoulder bag and passed it to Hettie. The box was beautifully decorated with snow cats playing in a winter scene.

'That's lovely!' said Tilly. 'And look – you've called it The Tabby In White selection.'

'That's right,' said Dandy, 'just pure white chocolate with no additives!!'

THE END

Acknowledgements

Family dynamics and inheritance have always interested me, especially when we look back at the pioneering dynasties that have formed the basis of our everyday lives here in the twenty-first century. We can trace much of our progress back to the Victorian society and their thirst for innovation and change, but some of our simple pleasures like chocolate have had a lasting effect around the world in bringing joy to millions of people.

The Aztecs started it by producing a rather unpleasant drink but it was a Victorian family who made the idea palatable for the nation and beyond. Their innovative practices brought them money and power, and it's these issues I have explored in *The Tabby in Black*. The Catberrys are, of course, characters of fiction, but offer an important nod to the past and indeed to the future.

I would like to thank Abbie Headon, my fantastic editor, for her guidance and understanding of the world I have created; Catriona Robb for her eagle eye across the copy edits; Jason Anscomb for another fine cover design; and Pete Duncan and all at Farrago and Duckworth Books for their continuing support for the series.

A special thank you should go to Dr Peter Fordyce for his expert advice and help with some of Morbid Balm's conclusions; to Nicola for her love and encouragement; and to Betsey and Stanley, who never miss a chance to disrupt my keyboard by walking across it at the most crucial moments. Finally, to the readers who have entered Hettie and Tilly's feline world in belief and with such great affection for the characters and the lives they lead.

About the Author

Mandy Morton was born in Suffolk. After a short and successful music career in the 1970s as a singer-songwriter – during which time she recorded six albums and toured extensively throughout the UK and Scandinavia with her band – she joined the BBC, where she produced and presented arts-based programmes for local and national radio. She more recently presents The Eclectic Light Show on Mixcloud.com.

Mandy lives with her partner, who is also a crime writer, in Cambridge and Cornwall, where there is always room for a long-haired tabby cat. She is the author of The No.2 Feline Detective Agency series and also co-wrote *In Good Company* with Nicola Upson, which chronicles a year in the life of Cambridge Arts Theatre. A complete retrospective collection of Mandy's music entitled *After The Storm* has recently been released on Cherry Red Records.

Twitter: **@hettiebagshot** and **@icloudmandy**
Facebook: **HettieBagshotMysteries**

Preview

The Murders at the Black Cat Museum

Where were you on the day Ena Dabbit was murdered? Hettie and Tilly are brought in to investigate a spate of murders in the Town as past and present collide. Suspicion engulfs some of the most respected residents, as our feline duo delves into family secrets to catch a killer.

COMING SOON

Also available

The No. 2 Feline Detective Agency begins

Hettie Bagshot has bitten off more than any cat could chew. No sooner has she launched her detective agency than she's thrown into her first case.

Furcross, home for senior cats, has a nasty spate of bodysnatching, and three former residents have been stolen from their graves. Hettie and her sidekick, Tilly, set out to reveal the terrible truth. Is Nurse Mogadon involved in a deadly game? Has the haberdashery department of Malkin and Sprinkle become a mortuary? And what flavour will Betty Butter's pie of the week be?

In a haze of catnip and pastry, Hettie steers the case to its conclusion, but will she get there before the body count rises - and the pies sell out?

OUT NOW

Also available

Gunpowder, treacle and shocks

As All Hallows' Eve approaches, Hettie Bagshot of The No. 2 Feline Detective Agency has more than just a ghost and a warlock tart on her plate.

Upon discovering the body of Mavis Spitforce, Hettie and her trusty sidekick Tilly set out to investigate an old crime and a spate of new murders. Why was Mavis Spitforce dressed for Halloween? Can Irence Peggledrip really talk to cats from the spirit world? And what's the connection to the legend of Milky Myers, suspected of murdering his family on Halloween, longer ago than anyone can remember?

As the November fog closes in, can the tabby duo unearth the truth, and stop the murderer before they strike again – and will there be enough samosas to go round?

OUT NOW

Also available

Hettie and Tilly are on the case

The town is celebrating its first literary festival, and The No. 2 Feline Detective Agency has been hired to oversee security.

When the body of the most popular author, Sir Downton Tabby, is found in a secluded part of the grounds, however, Hettie and her faithful sidekick Tilly are plunged into crisis as a serial killer stalks the festival.

As the duo turn their attention to investigating the death of Downton Tabby, will there be an author left standing? Will Meridian Hambone sell out of her 'Littertray' t-shirts? And will there be enough crime teas to go around?

OUT NOW

Note from the Publisher

To receive updates on new releases in The No. 2 Feline Detective Agency series – plus special offers and news of other humorous fiction series to make you smile – sign up now to the Farrago mailing list at farragobooks.com/sign-up.